Gina Mercer grew up on bananas and beaches on the north coast of NSW. She was raised by four powerful women (her mother and three sisters). Gina's father was killed in a car accident a few months before her birth. Living in an all-female household gave her a strong aware-ness of what women can achieve, and how desirable it is to have women as companions. She developed an early addiction to learning which led her to spend many years at university acquiring three degrees. Gina is still at university in a sense, as she now works as a senior lecturer in the School of Humanities at James Cook University, Towns-ville. Gina has previously published two academic books (*Janet Frame: Subversive Fictions*, UQP, 1994 and *Post-graduate Research Supervision: Transforming (R)Elations* co-edited with Alison Bartlett, Peter Lang Publishers, 2001) as well as a volume of poetry, *The Ocean in the Kitchen*, Five Islands Press, 1999. *Parachute Silk* is her first novel. She currently lives with her partner and daughter in an overgrown garden and a semi-renovated house.

PARACHUTE SILK

*Friends, food, passion
a novel in letters*

Gina Mercer

SPINIFEX

Spinifex Press Pty Ltd
504 Queensberry Street
North Melbourne, Vic. 3051
Australia
women@spinifexpress.com.au
http://www.spinifexpress.com.au

Cover design by Deb Snibson
Typeset by Palmer Higgs Pty Ltd
Edited by Barbara Burton
Printed and bound by McPhersons Printing Group

National Library of Australia
Cataloguing-in-publication data:

Mercer, Gina, 1959- .
Parachute silk.

ISBN 1 876756 11 X.

1. Female friendship - Fiction. I. Title.

A823.3

The author has made every effort to contact copyright holders to obtain permission to reproduce excerpts from their work. However, the author would be happy to hear from any copyright holders who couldn't be reached prior to publication.

"This publication has been assisted as part of a joint initiative by the Commonwealth Government through the Australia Council, its Arts Funding and Advisory Body, and the National Council for the Centenary of Federation."

To my many sustaining friends,
including my family,
who inspired this book.

The first draft of this novel was written during a three-week residency at Varuna Writers' Retreat in 1998. I wish to thank the Queensland Arts Council/Everald Compton New Regional Writer Scholarship for this invaluable gift of uninterrupted writing time, as well as all the tireless staff at Varuna who make it such a productive space.

Dear Molly,

You ask for exuberance? On this computer, in my efficiency-green office? I'll do my best! The grey neatness of the technology seems so opposed to passion, eros, excitement but I'd be slack if I ignored your begging and blamed my tools, wouldn't I? You also ask why I'm not currently a lesbian. Well it's a long story and could be told in many ways. I thought we'd discussed my sexual past quite enough but I forget that there've been times when I haven't been very open with you, though there are still some stories I'm not ready to tell you. Maybe never will be — but to get back to your question — yes I have been in love with women in the past and I may be again. But what am I saying? I am "in love" with a lot of women right at the moment. I just don't happen to be sleeping in their seductive beds, stroking their backs, kissing their beautiful, whisker-free mouths. Audre Lorde rightly says that eros is so much more than the plasticised sensations packaged and sold to us as "the erotic". Eros, she says, is the nurturer of our deepest knowledge. The open and fearless underlining of our capacity for joy.

Let's look at you and me. Our relationship is passionate, even when we're not in the same place — like right now when you're living in the blue-with-cold mountains and I'm slushing round in the tropics. We don't even share the same weather. When we speak on the phone I may be drooping about with a damp sarong draped languidly round my heat-plump hips while you are wiry with the effort of keeping warm. How remote is that, in terms of shared bodily experiences? Our connection consists mainly of vibrations of sound travelling through kilometres of wire and plastic in a modern miracle of technology, but the technology isn't a match for the power of eros, passion and the exuberance of our sea-deep talk, is it? Any more the computer's disapproving Fifties-neat look is going to stop me writing as recklessly as I want to, she says with determination. And now I've turned off the "right justification" button it feels a whole lot easier.

The language of computers is amazing, isn't it? I mean, think about the connotations of *right justification*. Sounds like something obligatory in McCarthy era courts. And *word processor* — puts me in mind of processed cheese, the words coming out all flat and pale yellow, without a bitey taste or texture anywhere, know what I mean? But I digress again, or still, or maybe you can't digress if you aren't going in a single direction ... enough!

Anyway my lesbian past may still be my lesbian present and my lesbian future if you take lesbian in its widest possible sense — which may be a paradox to those who view my life and simply see a monogamous, hetero mother — but then as you know I'm heavily interested in paradoxes at present — they're my life! For a while I struggled to iron out my contradictions, like a good housewife getting rid of all the unseemly crinkles in my everyday "fabric". Then I read some words that made me stay the hand that held the iron and eventually, put it away for good. Myra Jehlen, god bless her crinkly unbleached cotton socks, suggests that instead of ironing out our contradictions, we join them. So I'm trying to embrace my contradictions. If I imagine them as standing waves, and surf in them, it feels a whole lot better than trying to flatten them down to lake-smooth surfaces. Just like the sites of friction being the sites of greatest pleasure in sex, yes?

Oh, all right, I'll get back to the story I'm supposed to be telling you. Once upon a time I was living lonely in London in a busy shared household of other Australians who were also lonely in London. One bloke had a friend of his coming to stay, and he warned me before she arrived that she was a lesbian. "Not that there's anything wrong with that", he said in a thunder-n-lightning voice masquerading as liberal. Well being nineteen and naive I wasn't sure what to do with this "fact" he'd given me, about her being a lesbian, so I just didn't think about it, not even to register any deep curiosity. So she arrived and we talked a lot and ate a lot and drank a lot and played tourists a bit when the gruesome February weather allowed us. And then on some mornings, when it was too cold even to contemplate outside activities and anyway we had hangovers to get over, we would badger-burrow back into her bed, with tea and toast and things to read and letters to write and conversations to have and body-warming hugs to repel the joint pains of cold mornings, and that's how I discovered what it meant to be a lesbian. "They" say it's "unnatural", but it felt so smooth and easy and simple, just part of the continuum of being women who liked one another. She was wary of being seen to "corrupt" me, and he of the thunder-n-lightning voice took her aside one night and asked her about her "intentions". God how we laughed about this in bed the next day, our bodies rippling until she ended up spilling hot milkless tea on her breasts which then of course required soothing balms to be massaged into them and if that was the world's idea of corruption, then I was very ready for it.

Here's a poem written around that period:

Cartwheels

shall we go all the way?
share complementary cakes at coffee shops
walk for days exchanging histories in the open air
drive long-distance mulling over miles and miles of stories
go to clear-of-people places
eat fruit
sunbake
cartwheel on the grass and watch
the secret counter-cartwheels our breasts make
read each others' poems
rewrite the world
try out recipes and revolutions
share beds cats persimmons
get to know each other
piece by gentle piece

best thing is
being women
we are bound less
the more we know —
(as eve knew)
the more there is to know

what do you reckon?
shall we go all the way?

Of course such indulgent pleasures couldn't last, and one morning while reading the local paper in bed she found me a job. So I was away lifesaving for many hours each day — watching all those pallid English bodies twitch in livid-blue chlorine, like sucked jellybeans in aspic. She got to thinking that maybe she'd go travelling in Europe which was after all what she'd come to this side of the world to do, not merely to travel in bed with 19 year old first-timers. So she set off for Greece, on one of those Thomas Hardy days, you know the sort where you stood frozen:

> ... by a pond that winter day,
> And the sun was white, as though chidden of God,
> And a few leaves lay on the starving sod;
> They had fallen from an ash, and were grey.

I read that poem in my first year at university, a year of much grey-buried grief and chidden depression and it's stuck. It was that kind of day when my first woman lover left for Greece and I was left feeling very grim, washing the sheets, re-making the beds, and developing a kind of ashy identity crisis about the fact that I too was now a lesbian and how would I re-make my sense of me? The man with the warnings and worries about "intentions" made room in his working misery to take me out to lunch to a wonderful Chinese cafe in Soho to stir around this ashy mess of grief and puzzlement, which was very sweet of him, but we didn't get very far. How could we, when he saw being a lesbian as a problem and I simply saw it as fun? Now I don't think I've even come close to explaining how I went from this place of contradictions to the contradictions I'm currently surfing but it'll have to wait because I've got someone here to see me and that paper to send off and if I get too exuberant too early in the day I may very well lose my job! Until the next one —

Love
Finn

January 27

Dear little Finn

What a cute nineteen year old! Buxom and blooming and so innocent. I wouldn't dare call you 'little Finn' if you were close by but as you're thousands of miles away I'll be bold! It's what I do best, after all. And may I be so bold as to say that I think your first woman lover was pretty damn stupid? Fancy finding you a job when you'd already found a satisfying occupation – in her bed – and then to boot scoot out of that bed to go tripping round Greece. I mean, just what did she think she'd find there, to compare with the incomparable Finn? Hope she's done heaps of time on the 'starving sod' since then, sod her! Whoever she is. And I did just happen to notice that you skipped her name. So much for openness! You'll probably tell me that she's now some high-up government official, and you were being discreet in the interests of protecting the innocent. Can't say she did such a good job of that all those years ago, did she? Used the old 'pretend to spill tea on her breasts' trick, did she? Corny, except to the very very sweet and innocent. What a laugh, wish I'd been there. I read your letter out to Ania in bed last night. Yes it was bloody cold, at this time of year! And she had a lot of joint pains that needed repelling! We rippled around laughing under the doona. And that disturbed Leigh who was reading in bed next door – she's taking this HSC stuff so seriously – and it's only January! I don't know if we're all going to last the distance, especially if Ania and I can't even laugh in bed without it upsetting her – eleven months without laughing sounds fatal to me. As my mother used to say, people born without a sense of humour need a pension as much as anyone else born without some vital capacity.

Guess I'm rabbiting on a bit because it's been a shitty week here. The only good bit was getting your letter! Ania has been totally wrapped up, trying to get the year organised at her school. She's obsessed with 'being prepared'. And I thought she'd gotten over all those years in girl guides! Of course, she doesn't want another jumbled year like the last, but it'd be nice to spend some evenings slumped together on the couch watching telly, or looking at travel brochures or just any of the things couples do! And because there's shit between us, Leigh picks it up and gets all highly sensitive, so we can't enjoy ourselves without getting yelled at. Stuff it. It's weird. It's like she's suddenly being terribly tolerant and gracious about having a lesbian mother, but if her lesbian mother isn't a really 'good' mother, like some ruddy ad from the fifties, then she's free to kick up merry hell. Then I feel guilty for not being a nice neat nuclear mother, like all the other mothers she keeps raving on about. I'd really like to meet them, these ideal bloody mothers! You know any? What were you saying about enjoying contradictions? Wait until Lola's a teenager and I'll ask you then if you can still say you're enjoying them! No, but you have a point, and when I'm not feeling quite so tired and bitter I promise to have a good think about joining rather than scrubbing away at my contradictions. Me, I put the iron on the shelf a long time ago, not because of any smart theory. It just seemed better to give up on a bad job. So maybe if I take the next step and start to frolic in all the choppy waves surrounding me, I'll feel better. You reckon?

And to get back to the subject of your letter, no we haven't talked all that much about sex and your past lovers, or not enough to satisfy me. And now I want to know about the stories you won't tell! You know what my New Year's resolution is? To be a more voracious woman. No, but seriously, I got a letter from an old school friend who's organising a school reunion in October. I thought 'how quaint' and tossed it aside but then Ania got all interested, you know how she does, and asked if I'd twigged that it was a reunion to mark the twenty-fifth anniversary of our leaving school. Well of course I hadn't, and it came as a big shock. So that's what got me musing on our histories, on how we got from being neat little schoolgirls (isn't memory a marvellous tool for smoothing out contradictions?) to where we are now, and the more niggly question, where are we now? So you see my question about your past wasn't totally idle and voyeuristic, but more by way of trying to help me sort out some of my contradictions. I said sort, not iron. Maybe it's time to choose some that I'd like to surf in for a while, and to think about something other than – is there any bread for the cut lunches today? Or maybe to have something to occupy my vast brain while I'm cutting the lunches!

Speaking of which, Leigh'll be home soon and she wants a quick eat so she can go out with her friends at seven. So I'd better do a brisk imitation of your computer and look all neat and fifties instead of gossiping. Am sending you a poem we came across the other day. It seemed spot on, given the hot tea anecdote – enjoy. Don't begin to think that my voracious appetite has been satisfied by the story of the first lover. Look forward to your next.

Love you – Molly.

Breasts

is it ok
to write
about breasts
in this day and age
after all that men have
said and written and catalogued
on the subject or should i say object
of breasts? i don't know but i want to very
much because i feel wear carry them does that
make a difference? Kate thought so when she
wrote that hers stared back as interested
as a reporter i love that line the pert
reply to the bossy male gaze and
as i sit here with my breasts
blood-firm as any other
organ i want to
tell you about
the way it feels
to walk down my
garden with a sun-fresh
ripe paw-paw in hand and
a flesh-pushing breast in
the other and how i saw a woman
at a bus-stop (bust-stop) and how hers
hung at angles like the ears of a neglected
dog how i wanted to stroke them alert and make
her feel truly cherished as you do after a good breast
stroke and then there's the CWA woman hers make a
sandstone rock shelf shelter shelf in the land of cliffs
and the slender beach woman with fairy sandcastle breasts
with pale moon-pink shells on top and that swimmer who
has jelly-mould firms peaked with pecans becca reads of fig
breasted dancing girls as her own figs figure dance girlish
under the poet-shirt-front and Diana's wax and wane tender
full each month and remember the sumptuous sun-dried raisins
with plasticine tan at the Nice beach where the silicons bounce
light off fenders and the walrus woman with her sand-full
socks low-slung keeping her belly company in contrast
to the tight brace geometry bank clerk bet she wears
her bra to bed have you? can you imagine it? can
you remember trainer bras on your soft-new
shy shapes? or the tiny sacks of the blue-
haired breast-feeder we saw at the pub
band that time? big baby little breast
or the other way tiny baby fronts
huge ones with the milk just
down n out n leaking all over the place
and do you remember when we played that game of netball
in the change room you said I can squirt further than you
and the milk hits the other wall
slides down through the laughing full cream breasts
bouncing laughing moving flicking off the world

Dear Molly,

Was sorry to hear that things are less than creamy down your way. When Lola was younger she had a well-developed hermit fantasy. I still relate to it. She wanted to live on a farm, a long way from anybody, with only a cat and a horse for company. She didn't even want to have a phone. Said she'd spend all day riding round the hills on her horse, and all night snuggling up to the cat. What do you think? Sounds blissful, doesn't it? Do you think we could do a joint hermitship? Or is that too much of a contradiction? I was thinking we could live at opposite ends of a large patch of earth and run up flags if we wanted company. You're right, the theory of enjoying, or rather joining, contradictions sounds pretty flimsy in the face of the really big ones, like how to juggle your needs with those of your kids! But again I'm not answering your question, or your voyeurism. You can dress it up as a life crisis if you want to, but you're not totally convincing you know. Still — a twenty-five-year reunion does sound pretty daunting. Are you going — and taking Ania?? Whenever I hear about school reunions I always get torn. There's the absolute magnet of curiosity, I want to know how jerks like Joe Kirkham turned out, or what happened to interesting girls like Giovanna Azzopardi, etcetera. But then there's the horror of meeting all those old acquaintances. Having to go through the ritual of who's married, and how many kids, and what level income, and if you aren't married with 3 kids and a 6-figure income, "Why not? Where did you go wrong?" Yurk! A kind of "let's dump everyone on the normality scales and weigh them" game. You know how I hate normality! I know a woman who went back to a school reunion with her woman partner, and she said that "coming out" to her parents was 1000 times easier than that experience, the sports master made homophobic jokes in his speech and so on it went. But don't let that put you off, my darling! It'd be a brave or utterly stupid sports master who'd knowingly antagonise you and Ania. It could be fun, a kind of gossip fiesta. Go, just for me. I drool at the thought of the letters you'd write afterwards!

Well afterwards, in this story you want me to keep telling, when this first woman lover left for Greece, I muddled about with the grief and identity ashes for a while, and then buried them along with a whole lot of other messy stuff. I seemed to spend my whole time overseas running away. You know it's not uncommon amongst world travellers. All those smooth urbane cosmopolitan types are seething beneath the facade, hidden griefs as writhing lively as a mango full of fruit-fly maggots. The mango's full, fat, golden cheek may have only one tiny blemish, but pull back the skin, and the pale wriggling past bursts out and splats you.

But I'll continue ... I kept working at the swimming pool, guarding all those little English lives, terrorising the pool louts with a stern voice and me big muscles, as one of them commented when I threw him out. Drinking home-brewed cider with Welsh Jimmy in the Men's change room on late shifts and then heading off to the pub for a few pints before going back to my bleak, woman-less bed. Burials seemed so much easier when flooded with alcohol. Eventually I moved on, and travelled and worked a bit in different places, never finding anyone who could talk to me about all this. At one stage when I was seeking shared accommodation in London, I went to look at a place which advertised for "feminist women only". It was a bit of a shock. The house was in Brixton, very run down, and they explained that the plumbing was stuffed, but they'd made a household decision to leave it unfixed until they could find a woman plumber. And they had house rules about absolutely no men allowed, no brothers, fathers, gay men, nothing male, not even male pets — that's why the last woman left, she'd acquired a male dog. Well this was a piece of the lesbian continuum I'd never come across before, and I certainly didn't feel as if I'd fit in, what with my trainer-bra lesbianism and only slightly more lusty feminism. The women quizzed me about homosexuality laws in Australia. Well I didn't know enough about that to warm a nipple and they didn't ever ring me back. I assume they found someone else whose politics were powerful enough to help her rise above flooded bathrooms and leaking toilets. These days I'd probably have a better understanding of their radical position, albeit my hedonism might still baulk at the need for a woman plumber, but back then I simply felt bewildered and rejected and knew I hadn't found any kind of comfort zone. Finally I got back to Australia, older and a little more accomplished at the business of burying bad bits, and baring a more smoothly-moulded mango cheek for the world's inspection, and of course with a lot of terrific memories of other places and most especially, other places' foods. My entire travel diary from those years reads like a food tour of France, Spain, Norway, America, Greece, Canada, Britain and Sweden. Nothing much about my feelings, just details of what I was seeing and eating. Quite curious. Needless to say my body responded superbly to this and I weighed a splendid, Rubenesque seventy-five kilos when I returned — carrying my very own, very solid comfort zone.

Soon after I got back I received two phone calls. One was from Angus, an old acquaintance from my hometown. He'd heard through an ex-school teacher that I was back in the country, returning to study, this time at Melbourne Uni, and did I want to share a house with him and a couple of other uni students near there? Well, yes please was the obvious answer. Save going through the hassle of sifting through shared accommodation ads again. The other was from, have you guessed? The woman who'd deserted me in London for Mediterranean flights of fancy! She wondered if we could have lunch. Well, again the answer had to be, yes please. Even then I was a two-tone tart saying yes to both. The day of the lunch date I spent the morning in abject adolescent fluster about what to wear, and in the end, running late, I threw on a pair of jeans and a peasant-style embroidered shirt, which made me look like a blowsy twelve-year-old. Imagine how I longed to disappear into a drain beneath the rendezvous when I arrived, red-faced and at odds with myself, to see her there, yes, and waiting for me, but in the company of her long-term lover — definitely not part of the arrangement — or at least not part of the arrangement I'd made. I should simply have disappeared and not met up with them but, dutiful idiot that I was, I presented my foolish self for the most humiliating two hours imaginable. The long-term lover was a lean, rabbit-fit soccer player, who played for Australia. She'd never been anywhere near seventy-five kilos in her life. She obviously didn't believe my lover's story about our platonic London interlude — and used her formidable sardonic skills and older woman experience to show me up for a naive and undesirable fool! I crept home seeping tears onto the windowsill of the bus, of course I'd forgotten a hanky, and spent the next two hours in bed, soaked in feelings totally unrelated to joy!

I suspect there's nothing particularly lesbian about this experience, except that all the players in the scene were women. But let's face it, the Other Woman is the Other Woman is the Other Woman, as Gertrude Stein might have said if Alice B. Toklas had had an affair with an Other Woman and Gertrude hadn't had a thing about roses.

Now I feel miserable, just thinking about that event, thanks for nothing! And I'd better go or this timetabling nightmare I've been landed with will never get sorted. Hope you are all a little less barb-wired than last time,

Lots of love
Little Finn

splish splash splosh
ole Bobby put on his galosh
big bad thud
his galosh filled up with blood

Dear Molly,

Sorry about the ditty at the top, but I had to write it before I could do anything else this morning. Guess who's been making me feel homicidal lately? Yes, my new boss. He says he knows we won't have any trouble working together because he's heard such wonderful reports about my good will and support for my colleagues. Well have I got news for him! I have powerful good will towards a lot of colleagues but those who infantilise and patronise me are not among them. And the worst thing is that yesterday I was feeling so crabby about it, in spite of kicking hard over twenty fast laps of the pool (and imagining a certain body at the end of those kicks) that I yelled at poor Lola. Doesn't it just make you cramp up with guilt when you do that? And all because of this crackpot, temporary boss at my stupid job!! You are so right when you talk about mother-pain. It's a reality. What news of you and Leigh, speaking of mother-pain? Has she gotten over her sensitivities? You can't let her be precious the whole year or you'll go mad. What about organising for her to stay at some friend's house with a nice safe hetero set-up? One that you know to be particularly closed and miserable. That might put a dint in her reactionary fantasy about nuclear family bliss? But then again how can I pretend to give advice when my own mothering feels so utterly shobbly this morning?

I've slipped in some recent thinking on this, trying to make sense of some of it somehow.

Toad's Tongue

one childhood walk
my solo joy halted
witness
the cane toad
squatting huge
beside our bee hive —

as the bees emerge
rub-your-eyes-and-greet-the-day gentle
the toad's tongue
flicks and scoffs

now my rosy-bee daughter
leaps earlier than the sun
   walks solo
picks flowers over fences
eats the odd jewel mulberry
watches the world wake

restless
i listen for her return
remembering
the toad's tongue

Took me a while to recover after recovering that humiliating memory for you the other day. Didn't realise how much it still hurts! The swamp is a strange and fruitful place, isn't it? But there are some places I won't venture, even for you. Never know where the worms are writhing, do you, till you get there, take a step and end up with the sticky creatures inching up your legs. And then how to get them off?

Am sorely missing the sound of your laugh. Hope Ania's agitation and the reunion plans haven't got on top of you,

Lots of love
Finn

February 20

Dear Finn

Damn, it's nearly the end of February. I haven't done half
the things I wanted to get done before the year got into full
swing.

Was great to get your two letters so close together, though
I felt a bit guilty about not answering a bit faster. Can't
believe you felt so dutiful about keeping that lunch date,
even though your London lover turned up with her bloody
partner without warning. I know I wouldn't have stuck
around. I'd have shot into the nearest pub, gotten rotten
and sworn never to see her again. Just so hard for me to
imagine you as this compliant little good girl you describe
– doesn't fit with the woman I know. What happened to
you in the year after I left school, to make you so meek
and mild at nineteen? You were never the push-around type
at school as I recall. Anyway what went on after this
torturous lunch? Did you ever see her again? Or did you
take to sending her anonymous parcels of prawn-heads, to
match her stinky style?

No good reason why I was so slow answering your letter.
Perhaps I felt a little guilty about making you dredge up
unhappy memories. Maybe we could start up a dial-a-guilt
line, we're both so expert at it. People could dial us any
time of the day or night and we could take on their guilt
for them. It'd make about as much sense as the way we
carry on now, taking on guilt for every damn thing, even
when we couldn't possibly be responsible. Might even
make us some cash!

Life has become a bit quieter since last I wrote, though
Ania and I are still discussing the reunion in a half-hearted
kind of way. She's really keen to see where I went to school
and generally 'experience my roots' (any time honey, I say!)

... and I'm torn between curiosity and dread. Needless to say, Leigh is not keen to come with us. Can't imagine why! She did go to stay with a friend last weekend in a neat, straight household and had a horrible time ... but I plead total innocence, she really wanted to go. Apparently the food was awful, all freezer to microwave stuff. Both parents were very cool and remote, hardly spoke to the kids all weekend. The brother had a computer terminal attached to his brain, ate all his meals in front of the computer screen ... well that was her description. I said she must have been exaggerating. But perhaps she wasn't because she ate two large helpings of the veggie pie I made, and hit me with some solid cuddles the night she came home. That was only a few days ago, so it's too early to tell if this will have a lasting effect on how she views her deviant mother. But I've got all my fingers crossed.

Ania is, happily, a lot calmer now that the school year is properly under way. For a while there she seemed to be suffering from extreme pre-performance anxiety. I nearly got to the point of suggesting she have some counselling. And you know it must have been bad for me to even think of that!

Speaking of which, most of my clients are doing OK. They seem to have adjusted to my working from home at last. Some still display a gauche intensity about every detail of the therapist's life. Even some of the cool sophisticates get all ungummed when they discover that I read Kerry Greenwood, or that I use the same plant fertiliser as their ex-lover.

I'm still wrestling with terminology though. Even writing that earlier sentence made me uncomfortable. 'Client' sounds commercial or capitalist or something – too much like the lingo of lawyers or sex workers. In a newsletter from one of the counselling centres I used to work for, I noticed they now talk about 'consumers'. How accurate that seems some days when I end the last session feeling utterly drained and consumed. But that's not every day, thank goodness. Or should I thank my healthy sense of self-preservation and Ania's steady income, which allows me the luxury of having one that fluctuates a little. So I don't see 'consumers' as being my term of preference. Then again, do I hang up my shingle as a 'psychotherapist' with all the 'psycho-the-rapist' connotations it's acquired in recent years? Or 'psychologist' with its quasi-scientific ring?

I guess semantics like this seem pretty unimportant in comparison to the actual work (like how to help a nurse back to some sort of emotional equilibrium after her twenty-four month stint in a Rwandan refugee camp) but it does bother me. It's like there's no right word because there's no community recognition for the work I do. And maybe I shouldn't have a mini-identity crisis about terminology. But it seems significant that there's no accurate term for the emotional healing – without drugs, pseudo-science or imperialism – that women like me do. So there.

Phew! Where did all that come from? I certainly didn't sit down to rave to you about what I call myself or those who come to speak with me, but there you are. Hope you had a cup of coffee on hand to see you through it. That's one of the things I love about writing to you – I never quite know where I'll end up. But don't think you can use the same excuse when you write back. I've set you an agenda and I expect you to address it (as well as the envelope) – or else – she says through fascist-neat teeth. I'd better go. My next client, consumer, explorer or seeker-of-health arrived early, and that was ten minutes ago, so I'd better stop with the chat, or she'll be defining herself as an im-patient – and I wouldn't like that.

Love to you all – Molly.

Dear Molly,

Well, I'm at the computer already and it's only 5 a.m. Must be something wrong with me. Well there is, actually — the sausages I ate last night. They were so full of preservatives that I felt crook all night. Dreamt about penguins wearing floaties, black and white floaties of course, so that the skuas and leopard seals couldn't see them. See what a combination of nature documentaries and children's puzzle books has done to my unconscious? The other thing that pricked me out of bed was the feeling that I ought to reply to your letter. It arrived a while ago but I find myself mulling it over all the time — and not always calmly.

Yes, I do think semantics count, though obviously they're not the only work we need to do. Immediately after getting your letter I went back to reading a student's work and she was talking about the way women's work and experiences aren't properly recognised and named. Reading your letter reinforced her point. Maybe the current mainstream does have trouble imagining the kind of work you do. Maybe you need to tap into your creative self and help it along with a few new words. Could take a while for them to gain currency — but then Delphi didn't get famous in a day, did it?

The second thing that's been making me restless was the last bit of your letter. It's been nosing around the back of my brain like the large slow silverfish nosing round my desk this morning looking for something to chew. What bothered me (see silverfish decide which page it's going to maul) was that you seem to feel you've got the right to set the agenda for this correspondence. I know you chucked in the obligatory self-aware therapist's joke about fascist teeth to show that you were pushing me and knew it, but you still went ahead and did it. Well SORRY but one cute little joke doesn't wipe the slate clean and buy submission from this little black duck. I mean, what's the fascination with my past relationships? Do you and Ania get off on it? Is it some quaint voyeuristic fillip to your lagging sex life? There's a whole genre of pornography where men get off watching lesbians. Is this the same? Am I, the bisexual, your exotic other who can write you erotic stories every so often and make you ripple under the doona with laughter and just a tint of worldly-wise contempt for my naivete? I hate the term bisexual. Like so many words we have to use it's a misfit. But I also hate the thought of being used, especially by you. If you're going to set an agenda at least be explicit about who's at the meeting and what the meeting's about. And speaking of agendas, what about my right to not comply with yours? Or even to set them for myself? Had you thought of that? I've hinted at it before, but I'll be right up front now, as that seems to be the only way of getting through to you. There are some stories that I just won't tell. So no matter how much you wheedle or wiggle the thumbscrews, it's not going to happen!

Getting angry early in the morning on an empty stomach is a weird experience! Guess I'm feeling pretty shitty about all this because I feel women, including some of my best friends, feminists, have fallen into a trap with regard to sex. It's become so all-important, as Cora Kaplan says, nowadays sexuality is the text while power is the sub-text that always wears the fig leaf. Feel a lot of women get all hung up on whether or not I'm a lesbian (and that's another term it's hard to define) — but sex is just one aspect of me. I don't want to be defined by my erotic preferences, I don't want to be confined in a label generated by what I lust after. I love my vulva dearly, it's given me hours of pleasure, but so have many other parts of my body, like my stomach or my brain. But people don't feel they know everything about my personality when they discover that I have a passion for baked potatoes or ripe mangoes, do they? Or if they find out what I like to read and think about? They might feel they know me a little better but they couldn't say with definitive certainty, oh she's a bit flaky politically, she's a potato-eater or poetry-reader?

Would your agenda for this correspondence have yielded more interesting results if you'd asked about my reading history? I've slept with quite a lot of people, I'll admit, but I've read a zillion times more books. Think about it.

I must go and get myself some breakfast and I can hear Lola stirring so she'll soon be at my elbow requiring a hug and a slice of raisin toast. Hope you haven't read this on an empty stomach. I really didn't get up in the dawn to fight with you. Did I? I don't think so. Anyway I love you and look forward to your next.

Unprickly hugs
Echidna Finn

March 10

Dear Finn

Luckily I didn't read your letter until I'd mellowed a little over a couple of whiskies (a legacy of my parents' last visit) and a good dinner. Must say your anger came as a surprise. But then I could sort of see what you're getting at. I've been thinking about it for a couple of days now. Don't know if I've quite come to grips with it, but thought I'd better write back quickly. If I know you, there were probably a host of unlovely feelings that leapt on you the minute the letter was posted. I know that's what always happens to me when I post a less-than-friendly letter to anyone. Now I'm sorry if that sounds too much like the all-knowing therapist predicting your emotional landscape. Your letter has made me more careful about what I write – which may be a useful thing – if it increases my awareness rather than my writer's block. Anyway I was concerned about what you said and felt. Please don't eat any more of those sausages if they wake you up so bilious. Lord, I'm sounding more and more therapeutic by the minute – sorry. I'll try a new paragraph, maybe that'll get me out of therapy mode and down to business.

I didn't consciously set out to set an agenda for you. The goddess knows what my unconscious had in mind, and I'm not going to a therapist to find out!! I really did just want to talk to you, as a deep friend and thinker, about the erotic, and sexuality. How it gets decided in a life. You've crossed certain boundaries in your life – in all sorts of arenas, you're right – and I love you dearly for that talent, as well as the way you talk about life. Well that's what made me begin to ask you to write about this stuff. Maybe it sounds kind of simple and dorky when I put it that way, but it's really how it is/was. Whatever.

Your notion that Ania and I were somehow exploiting you as an 'exotic' sexual object sounds like the sausages talking for all the sense it makes to me. Guess I found that the shittiest part of your letter. I'd have thought that you could trust me absolutely in that, and every other, respect. I feel bewildered by the mood that could bewitch you into such paranoid fantasies – Ania and I as porno queens? Come on! Does that sound falsely reassuring? It shouldn't, and if it does it may only be that I'm trying to restrain my anger from trampling across the keyboard. I want to tell you, with absolute clarity, that Ania and I have a VERY wonderful sex life, without the necessity for any tidbits from your past. Really!

Well, I was going to write that when we got through this, maybe we could get back to that absorbing discussion of semantics and sex that we were having before you ate the sausages and woke up before it was good for you. But there I go setting agendas again. I can see it's a bad habit that you're going to break me of, or make me break. Please do keep writing about whatever you want, my sweet one, only keep writing. And of course you don't have to tell me all. My voracity can and will respect your silences, I promise. I can even handle your anger and regard it as something that helps me to learn – I think – well I can as long as the whisky lasts.

Re-reading this I can see all kinds of tricky bits, which your eye might catch on. But if I go on revising it until it's 'right', you'll think I'm so furious that I'm never going to reply, or worse, that I've stopped loving you. So my concern for you overrides my desire to make this the perfect reconciliation letter. Here it is complete with warts.

Love always – Molly.

Dear Molly,

Well, thanks for the fast-track reply to my less than loving missive, and I haven't poked holes in it, but read it as I'm sure you wrote it, with sincerity and integrity — and a stomach full of home-grown pawpaw dressed in lime juice, instead of half-digested meat dressed in chemicals. And you'll be pleased to hear that it's not 5.30 a.m., but a civilised 9.30, Lola is safely (?) at school and I'm working at home, so I can't be constantly interrupted by students and colleagues.

Since becoming a mother I've become used to living on small amounts of interrupted sleep and working in tiny bites of interrupted time, but I can't say that I like it — it's not only the coitus that's interruptus these days — it's bloody everything. What worries me is that I might become so used to it that when it's no longer imposed by Lola and her needs, I'll be so habituated to it I won't be able to operate any other way. I heard a guy talking on the radio the other day — he treats insomnia — and he said that one of the major groups that come to see him are women who become so inured to broken nights when their children are young, that fifteen years after their kids have left home they're unable to achieve an ordinary night's sleep. That thought horrifies me. You've been working as a mother longer than I have. Has that happened? Are you able to sleep through now, or does Leigh keep you up at night for other reasons? Or have you been able to revert gratefully to your pre-daughter days and sleep eight hours in a row and only work in four-hour blocks? I begin to weep as I list such possibilities. They seem so utterly unlikely, and yet I know lots of childfree people who regard such things as boring and ordinary, not as unattainable luxuries. How I wish I could make them grateful for their wealth! It seems so crazy the way our time gets organised — here I am racing round like a rat on crack trying to do all the necessary jobs, and yet my neighbours, all over seventy, complain that they're drying out with boredom and a lack of feeling necessary to anyone — is there any way this could get balanced out, so that women like me don't die from having too much to do and the people next door don't die from having too little?

Guess I'm prattling on about fairly neutral stuff because it feels safe, and right now, between us, that's probably a good thing. And also because I've been in a bit of a slide for the past few days. You know how I get every six months or thereabouts? So plumb tired that I desperately hope I won't wake up again. It's not a good space to be in and I roundly chastise myself for being self-indulgent and ungrateful for all the richness in my life, and ask myself why I'm making such a fuss when I only have one child at home, and most women in the world do it much tougher than I do and ... but none of that seems to impinge on the tsunami of desire, the longing to sharpen our little boning knife and use it to let out some of the exhaustion and cut myself a shimmering skein of uninterrupted sleep. This is how I wrote about it one slab-grey day, about six months after Lola was born:

Red on Grey

i know a rock – it has a view of the sea
i feel it waiting, waiting for me
on the flat grey rock i'd hold a picnic spare
just a bottle and a knife
one for easing care
one for ceasing life

there'd be red on the rock
when the running feast ends
just the ticking bush clock
as the red quietly wends

a final tracing of red on grey
and a body gone out
on a rockshelf
                    above the bay

Pathetic, isn't it? The cliched rhyme reflects my sense
that this desire, this option is overly simplistic, predictable,
a lack of imagination masquerading as tragedy. Maybe that
sounds harsh but with all the suicidal tendencies and
violent ends in my family tree, I need to instil a bit of
tungsten in my spine when these sodden-nappy feelings
threaten to engulf me. I don't remember you ever talking
about feeling this way. Do you ever? Or do you feel too
ashamed to mention it, even to me, a friend to you-the-
woman, not to you-the-therapist? Or maybe you're better
organised and able to care for yourself so that you don't
get into such a mollobby mess. Or maybe you don't have
quite so many half-decayed skeletons in your cupboards as
I seem to ... I don't know.

Angus says I need to get past the old story imposed on
me by that child molester. But it runs so deep. I see
definite traces of it in things like my habit of looking after

everyone else's needs before my own. I wait till mine are hammering at the door in such a monstrous riot that neither Angus nor I can see a way of accommodating them without being completely overrun and overwhelmed. It's such a powerful story to imprint on a tiny child. It's kind of engraved in my body and psyche. I mustn't cry out at pain because it might cause too much bother to those around me. Their needs for gratification, or for quiet no-trouble-at-all girls, are the primary concerns. That was the message scored into my flesh and although Melina and I did all that good work, years ago, uncovering the wounds, cleaning out the festering muck and soothing them with healing balms, the scars still remain — like ancient plot-lines — and sometimes I plod along those old traces like a worn-out pit pony. A rather imbecilic pit pony who can decipher untrustworthy motives in even the oldest and most loving friend. It wasn't just the sausages which talked in that angry letter I sent, but also that molested me, the one who learnt to suspect all, even those, or perhaps especially those, who wore the mask of affection. Of course I know that your affection has never been a mask, but every now and then, the trip-wire gets tripped and I lash out at, almost as if I have to test, the people who do love me, to make sure that this time it's not a fake. Sorry. I guess I tell you all this, not by way of any kind of excuse, but simply because that is what happens and I hate it, and fight it, but it still does happen every now and then. And that's why I appreciated your fast track and reassuring response. Thank you.

Better go, I have to show my face at work sometime today. Hope this finds you all well, rested and hilly (as opposed to depressed).

Lots of love
Finn

April 19

Dear Finn

It's taken a while to get back to you. Life's been a cyclone.
I don't admit to being a control freak but the intensity of
these emotional gales has had me struggling. And it was
extra frustrating because I wanted to reply fast to your last
letter, and that poem.

Was it a muted plea for help? Why can't you simply yell out
loud when you're hurting? Your strong woman act is
convincing to most of us, most of the time but I think
you're still trying to be the quiet no-trouble-at-all daughter,
mother, partner, friend, worker and every other bloody
thing, aren't you? Well just stop it. When you feel rotten,
pick up the phone and talk to me. I don't care if you cry
for an hour, or sound pathetic, or feel it might not be a
good time to trouble me, or any of those other feeble
excuses you trot out whenever we have this conversation.
Just call. It's not hard, is it? Sorry, I know I'm sounding a bit
harsh, and maybe I'm giving advice through fascist teeth
again when I said that I wouldn't. But hey, Finn. This ain't
the time to muck about being nice. And if you didn't want
this kind of response, why'd you send me that damn poem?
It's been giving me nightmares. And not just because of the
ghastly rhyme scheme. If you have the wit to calculate a
suicide, and formulate a cute little poem about it, then
surely it's not too complex to pick up that old technology,
the telephone, and dial the number of one of your oldest
friends? Is it? Huh?

Heard a much better poem at a reading the other day,
about women writers and suicide, I'll see if I can get hold
of a copy to put in this letter. Anyway, one of the reasons
for not getting back to you sooner, and for my somewhat
tetchy response, is that Leigh's been really tricky lately. And

anything that affects a daughter comes round as guilt and storm for her mother, doesn't it? Earlier in the year, remember I told you she was being very 'sensitive', a bit precious about anything Ania and I did which might affect her HSC preparation? Well we talked through that one, and finally made a deal about 'house rules' (true!) to suit all of us. And we discussed the fact that three adults sharing space needed to work stuff out, whether they're a hetero couple and teenager or a lesbian couple plus teenager or any other combo you can think of. All pretty standard stuff, a bit tense at times, but seemed to be sorting out OK. We'd have the occasional fireball fight when we were all pre-menstrual at the same time – that was fun – but predictable and bearable. But what's happening now is impossible.

She's shutting me out all the time. She won't talk. I can stand almost anything except complete silence, which she damn well knows. None of my normal strategies work. She goes to her room to study and just stays there. Won't come out for meals. The other day I found she'd actually pissed in a jar in her room, so she didn't have to come out to go to the toilet, didn't want to run the risk of bumping into me. Shit it hurts.

Am feverishly reading the advice manuals every night, getting up stare-crazy every morning. And you guessed it, each book gives completely conflicting advice. Some suggest that this kind of behaviour is designed to attract attention, and if ignored will lead to suicide attempts, so one must give more attention, love, care and so forth. But there's precious little practical stuff on how to achieve this. Pat the slammed bedroom door for five hours every day, like you do the hand of someone in a coma in the desperate hope that they'll know you're there for them through all the hardwood barriers?

Other books say this is normal behaviour, especially in teenagers with 'smothering' or 'over-protective' mothers. What the hell does 'over-protective' mean? It's so bloody hard to protect your kids as it is ... and one slip in the protection and you're 'neglectful'. Really, who'd be a parent? Anyway this species of advice book tells me to stand back and let Leigh find her own feet, give her lots of space, gently let her know that I respect who she is, no matter how different to me she wants to be. As if we hadn't discussed difference and tolerance enough in this queer little household of ours.

My instinct is to grab her and hold her in a tight, full-length body hug till it's all better, but I know she's not a two-year-old with a scraped knee any more. What does a mother do when she thinks, or the experts think, that her mother-love is the cause of her child's problems? I feel completely stuck, can't think straight, or even creatively queer, on this one. And to cap it all off, this colleague whom I trusted, I mean I supported him big-time when his marriage nearly cracked open last year. Well, when I mentioned all this to him, hoping for support and maybe even some helpful advice, my desperation loud enough for anyone to hear, he suggested that it was probably all due to the abnormal parenting to which Leigh had been subjected. It was so hard not to king-hit his smug, urbane, wrinkle-free face. I was so shocked, and disappointed that I didn't have the wit to quote him the stats on youth suicide in rural areas where the hetero norms are stringently adhered to, nor all the clients he and I see, year after year who are completely stuffed in the head as a result of 'normal' parenting, nor did I mention the number of suicides and 'accidental' deaths caused by the ongoing effects of incest in so-called normal families. I know you know all this stuff but I need to talk to someone ... am taking some of my own advice for a change.

Want to talk for a couple more hours or millennia but Leigh's agreed to see a doctor at the Women's Health Centre. I'm so ruddy desperate I'm hoping it's just her hormones. I'm to drive her there in ten minutes ... so I'll stuff this in an envelope and post it while I wait outside for her. Send me something inspirational or frivolously distracting in your next one ... please ... sorry if that sounds like I'm setting an agenda. I am. Unashamedly. I need your gentle loving words and arms around me right now, to stop me falling over.

Love and a few howls — Molly.

PS I did find that poem in the end.

Late Night Critique of Sexton and Plath

All week the mad dead have circled my sleep, creeping
off the pages I read while I rocked my child, fever-flushed
and inconsolable. I asked them why;
why wasn't it enough; the weight of a child
the smell of rain, the comfort of unread books?
The child banged his head on my shoulder —
we raged together, dumbly persistent in our pain.
I hated them for giving in, leaving their lives
a sad pile of pickings for the greedy.
And how we excuse them, write their absent notes,
wipe their faces clean, make them tidy.

In the dark room the dead assembled,
they held out their hearts
like begging bowls but I would not love them.
If I'm called to give witness it's not to that —
death as a blanket, a comforter
but how life takes over, bustles in
opens the curtains,
gives the day a shake.

Dearest Molly,

Well, I'm only too happy to try to rise to your agenda, if I can. Hoping desperately that some silky words can bring comfort to you right now — cobwebs anchoring in a cyclone. How hard this one is. What happened at the doctor's? Did Leigh find it useful? Can just imagine the scene afterwards, you waiting (never your favourite occupation), then panting like a puppy to know how it all went, hungry to lick over every nuance and phrase of the doctor-daughter dialogue for the taste of helpfulness, but cat-conscious of Leigh's right not to tell you a damn thing, if she so chose ... what happened?

After I got your letter, I felt tempted to ring the airlines to see if there were any seats available for me to fly straight down to see you ... but I wasn't sure, after a moment's thought, whether that would be the most useful thing to do, would it? Please tell me if it would help. Or would Leigh like to come up here for the school holidays? I know my credibility with her might be a bit shaky because I'm your friend but sometimes, trusted aunt-figures are just what a young woman needs. Similar enough to a mother to be comforting but definitively not mother at the same time. I know my mum's sister, the elegant Aunt Alethea, was an invaluable and challenging listener for me when I left home and was wallowing badly in the backwash of my final couple of years at school. Should I ring Leigh and suggest she come up? Or would it best come from you? I won't take any action until I hear from you. Why don't you ring me? Any time would be fine, you know that. And how is Ania handling all this? She's usually wonderful in a crisis, how I hope that she's able to be your quilt comforter, and not grappling some crisis at school that distracts and drains her. Of course, if any, or all of you, want a tropical retreat please don't hesitate to let me know. Enough, sounds trite, but whatever I can do, you know I will.

Now you asked for distractions ... I'll see what I can do. In one of those curious coincidences which lace our friendship, the day your letter arrived, I'd started work on a poem on the ludicrous nature of optimism, want to hear it? She asks rhetorically, although I know if you're really not in the mood for such things, you can just slip it back in the envelope and pour yourself a strong whisky.

Here's the poem:

'Tearing things to pieces to sew 'em together again'

'O mother,' said Maggie ...
'I don't want to do my patchwork. ... It's foolish work ...
Tearing things to pieces to sew 'em together again.'
Maggie Tulliver in *The Mill on the Floss*, George Eliot, 1860, (p.61)

i'm glad to live in this chaotic century
escaping the corsets that worsted poor maggie

maybe she's right about quilting
facile repetition fashioning
mental circumcision

yet i've a savage urge
to tear things to pieces and
patchwork them into poems

i host the ridiculous impulse of optimism

each day approach the letterbox
    heart murmuring
today there'll be a package from that friend
    whose words spring my mind
    like a spade refreshing soil at winter's end
a missive from one of my several sisters
welcome as a hand on my morning-fresh breast

the blind rhizome of hope noses damply
through the dank soil of ordinary days

yes, i get the mizzle of reality across my face
but hear an ebony voice
touting hope as the radical root of revolution

see — radicals are simply optimists
baring their nubbly neck-thin desires above
the tundra of The Normal
letting the world laugh at their desires
to grow something generous and tree-tough
like votes for women and blacks
weren't they once rickety ideas?
now rain-trees in the garden politic
    that no-one dares to prune

and i look at the compost

    all those witless words
    toppled hopes
    mouldy desires

see — they all get dug in
embracing deeply
combusting like fetid family life
until they mulch and merge
comforting as a glove
    nurturing
        some rhizome
        some radix
some hope full root

Well when you asked for distractions perhaps an ode to
Maggie Tulliver and the compost was not quite what you
had in mind, but then again you have said you enjoy my
capacity to surprise. Of course the spade-refreshing friend
is you, you always make me feel less lumpen, no matter
how long my mental winter has lasted. Guess this poem
sprang from a number of sources but one is a real concern
about the prevalence of depression. You know how it has

raddled my sister, May, for years, and sculpted my poet friend to desperate fragility, and recently it dumped on one of my talented students, and all the experts on the radio reckon it's going to become more and more common over the coming years. And although you carefully, or fearfully (?), didn't use the word in describing Leigh, I guess that fear is what's driving your manic reading and worrying. Yes? Am I right? So I could rush out and buy us both shares in the company that makes anti-depressants, but you know me, I'd rather write a poem about hope. Because depression ... isn't it simply the absence of hope? Oh, I know it's never simply any one thing, but when optimism goes missing, that's when we really start to desiccate, isn't it?

I'm going to post this on my way to pick up Lola, so I'll stop, but I'm thinking of you and Leigh —

Love you
Finn

April 30

Dear Finn

Just went for a walk in the garden and the trees are doing their magnificent and predictable chandeliers of autumn routine. Beautiful and inspiring. You'd love it, and probably write a poem about it. But right now I'm not in the mood for the joys of nature, or your poetry for that matter. I know you were trying to be helpful but did you really have to send that letter? It was so chock full of homespun cliches I almost threw up. Next, you'll be knitting jumpers out of recycled muesli. First you suggest, 'let's all take a happy family holiday' ... like that's going to fix anything. And then that poem, full of tree roots and compost. Yeah, right. You reckon all I need to do is love the contradictions in my life, have a little play in them and then when I'm done, start meditating on the compost? Stuff that for a joke. You aiming to get voted Best Little Miss Tropical Hippy? What have you been smoking lately?

S'pose your letter was one step up from my smug and critical colleague, but only by one degree of ultra-smug. Why didn't you throw in a poignant description of those big butterflies you're always raving about? And what about a couple of rainbows? Now there's an original metaphor for hope. You missed that one. That would have made all the difference. Would really have set me up for some inspiration. I'd have completely forgotten my worries and started to sing the Hallelujah chorus, day in, day out.

Next time you think you're super-sophisticated because you've 'DISCOVERED' some simple truth, don't bother bloody telling me about it, OK? I need that kind of solace right now, like I need treatment for my 'unnatural' sexuality.

I don't need to be told to be 'optimistic'. I'm real glad if it works for you, in your cosy, safe, tropical garden, but sing it somewhere else. Maybe you could print off a poster, with that bewdiful poem set against a tasteful pastel rainbow background, and make a squillion, like that inspirational guru, Helen Steiner Rice. She must be dead by now, you couldn't produce so many nauseous cliches in one lifetime and expect longevity too. She probably died of stomach cancer at thirty-six. So there's your opening. You'll thank me for making this suggestion one day. See how optimistic I can be? I'm making such an effort to take your good advice, and to cheer up, look on the bright side, see the silver lining in the compost heap. Yeah right.

Not going to write any more. You're not going to love this letter and I think I've made my point. Don't ring. I don't feel like calmly and sensibly discussing this, resolving it ... taking responsibility for my part in it etcetera ... Maybe the most inspiring thing about that poem was the bit about tearing things to pieces. But I agree with Maggie, quilting is a stupid idea. So don't go trying to patch things up with me for a while. I'm just not in the mood for careful stitching. I have other uses for my needles at present.

Molly.

7th May

Dear Molly,

What can I say except, sorry? Platitudes and the giving of "good" advice seem to be sins I'm particularly prone to committing. Won't pretend that your words didn't hurt, felt like a rampant nail gun had attacked me, and I'm still picking nails from certain tender spots. That crack about Steiner Rice was the most effective. But, such matters are probably furthest from your mind right now. Mainly wrote to let you know that your letter had arrived, and made its mark, in case that information gives you some kind of bitter satisfaction. I do, in spite of all the spite, still love you, though I'm not big on forgiveness right now. And I'd still like to be able to help out in some way, if you could suggest anything that wouldn't seem offensively smug, self-righteous or cliche-craven to you. I'm taking your advice, and won't pick up the phone. Think the needle is firmly in your groove.

Contact me if you think it worthwhile, or if you want to talk, or laugh even. No, I guess that'd be way too cheerful and optimistic, sorry. Take care, and give my love to Leigh and Ania.

Regretfully
Finn

Look Finn, I'm sorry. I love you and your words, most times. Still not up to calm discussions. Am trying to work out what's going on but failing miserably. Know it's asking a lot, but could you write to me, on any topic other than hope, children, mothers, or compost – please?

I think, maybe even hope (!) that I'll come back to a space where I can talk to you about what's happened, happening ... but I know I'm not there yet. In the meantime, send me a sign of some sort to let me know I haven't savaged our friendship beyond repair. Please. And did I remember to say I'm sorry?

Molly.

Dear Molly,

Well if I'm little Miss Tropical Hippy then I reckon you must have earned the title of Commandant Icebloch by now. Yes, you've been setting agendas again, and like a doltish, forgiving hippy-type person, I keep trying to comply with them. Really don't think this is healthy but I can see that now is not the time to try to sort it out. You have bigger and uglier fish to grill in chilli, and I have a massive hangover. So I'll talk about that. Should be safe territory.

Still suffering the side effects of your nail-gun missive, I decided to clean out the freezer yesterday. You know how therapeutic martyred domesticity can be? Anyway, while I had my armpits in the ice and grot, thinking ever so warmly about our relationship, I found a tray of mango-cheeks, which we'd harvested off the tree in December. I convinced myself that they were absolutely past their freeze-by date and needed to be converted into mango daiquiris that night.

Picked up the alcoholic ingredients on my way to collect Lola from school, and by the time Angus came home from work, I had the glasses chilled, and frosted with sugar, and the blender jug full of golden-orange liquid ice. See how obsessive I become when I'm strung out? Almost plucked my eyebrows before he arrived so I'd look the complete 1950s loving wifey ... but I've still got my hippy reputation to sustain, so I restrained the tweezers, for now.

The idea was that we'd drink a couple and then refreeze the remainder for some other night when we needed a shot of Vitamin C. Well you can guess what happened to that bright resolve. The jug full rapidly became the jug drained and dreggy. A rather unco-ordinated dinner happened sometime in the course of the evening. Lola got to go to bed late because we couldn't be bothered arguing with her, and we went to bed feeling languidly sensual, as well as very witty, in a sort of mango-lit haze. But this morning life has a rather different hue, and I've put a notice on my office door, saying, "Please Don't Disturb". I'm hoping all my colleagues and students think I'm deep in thought, immersed in my latest research project. And I am in a way ... researching deep into my desk drawers to see if there are any more pain killers lurking behind the envelopes and notepads. Being the kind and loving friend that I am, I'm enclosing the recipe for the daiquiris. Have a vague recollection that you asked for a copy of it after your last visit. Remember that night we sat on the verandah, eating the prawns Angus cooked and drinking these? But perhaps that's coming perilously close to discussing our collective composted past ... so I'll move on. Here's the recipe. Another friend of mine (yes, I do have other long-distance friends) who lives in Melbourne, successfully made these by buying tinned mango, freezing the cheeks the night before and then proceeding to mix as per the recipe. Maybe, you could ask Ania to get all domestic and do that for you, to cheer you up, or maybe, here's a radical idea, maybe you could do it for her one night. Set and then comply with your own agenda for a change!

Mango Daiquiris

1 ripe mango or small tin of mango pieces
120 ml (4 oz) white rum
45 ml (1½ oz) white curacao
20 ml (1 oz) fresh lime juice, be more generous
    if you like it sharp
1 teaspoon caster sugar
Half a cup of ice cubes

Peel and slice mango. Place all ingredients in blender and blend until smooth. Pour into chilled cocktail glasses, and consume joyously. Makes 2 or 3 generous cocktails.

As you may remember, it's a glorious way to get smashed, and I'm sure all those vitamins and minerals make the toxic aftershock less damaging to your liver. Well that's my hippyish theory ... and I'm sticking to it. Won't go on any longer, my small stock of generosity towards you, and my ability to focus on the computer screen through this headache are rapidly diminishing. As a last gesture towards what I hope (it's such a persistent impulse) will be the less turbulent future of our friendship, I've enclosed a piece I wrote recently about one form of solace which I find reliable... and which I hope you won't find offensive. There's not a single mention of compost, or even anything natural. Hope it makes you feel, well if not cheerful, maybe just a little daiquiried.

Cheers
Finn

My Bed Every Time

Beds are amazing spaces — all kinds of things can happen in them, on them, around them, under them. A lot's been written about them, but only as incidentals, you know, as the obligatory backdrop in a 'bedroom scene'. There hasn't been much in the way of a good look at the bed itself. So let me introduce my main character here — my bed.

My bed doesn't have a name. Does yours? Nah, too cute, like naming your car or something. But let me tell you straight away, I'm deeply in love with my bed. It's high and it only ever wears thick, white, pure cotton sheets. You see it's rather queenly in disposition — and queen size. When I come home, sore from encounters with friends, work, lovers, enemies, the world — or just plain tired — my bed's always waiting for me — a clean, clear, white space calmly there — to take, without question, my weary body, to accept my groans and sweat and ecstasy and blood and inertia and tears and fantasies — as I lie or tangle in its comforting arms. And you know the best thing? It never gives advice.

You'll be thinking I'm only in love with its passivity, but my bed's more than a pretty space, it's a waterbed. I know — you're thinking "kinky", "sleazy" — aren't you? But my waterbed is neither of these things. It's firm yet giving — not sloshy and unpredictable like some waterbeds I've known. I must confess that sex is better on my bed than other beds. It always welcomes my lovers in. Unlike other loyal friends, my bed doesn't know the meaning of envy. It's much more accommodating to curves than most beds, and when an arm, or a leg, gets caught under a lover the limb isn't pinioned against a hard surface — the water in the bed simply glides aside to make a fitting hollow. So a long kiss isn't spoilt by your arm gradually losing sensation, moving through pins and needles to excruciation, until suddenly you pull out — bumping your lover's nose, grating your mutual teeth or biting your mutual tongues. These kinds of things don't happen in my kind of bed.

And another thing — it's always crispy dry and warm. Because the water has to be slightly heated, the sheets get lightly toasted too. In cold weather there's no risk of ankle-aching cold clutching at you as you wince between the sheets to lie there in one body-length cramp as you wait for the bed to be warmed by little old, little cold you. Or when it's been raining every day for three weeks and everything else in the house is mould-mottled and clammy, this bed miraculously provides dry, unclammy sheets so you don't wake up sticky and unrested. So — call me a sybarite, a hedonist, a spoilt hussy — but I love my bed.

So when someone says "Your place or mine?" there's no choice really — it's my bed every time.

June 26

Dear Finn

Thank you for your letter-package. 'Thank you' seems a
puny word to describe the way I felt when I wangled it out
of the post box. Firstly I was relieved to see a letter from
you at all. In amongst everything else I had this terror that
I'd damaged our friendship for always with my vicious
words. Then I felt dread ... what if this was the letter saying
don't bother me again? Sat in the car and read it in gulps,
like an alcoholic downing a first drink. And then I got all
weepy when I realised that it was like a really good
cocktail. Spiked with the pure spirit of your anger (quite
justified) and your hurt, but most of all with your one
hundred per cent proof love. It was so easy to guzzle, even
on a queasy stomach. I might just take your advice and
make Ania a jug full of mango daiquiri, and we can drink
it in your honour. God knows I should toast both of you for
putting up with me these past few months. Thank heavens
for generous women is all I can think to say. I know this all
sounds very soppy.

Just to let you know how off-the-air I feel, let me tell you
that I'm seeing a doctor about HRT next week. Yeah,
maybe it's my hormones that are the problem, not Leigh's
... or could it be a cruel combination of both? Anyway,
thought I'd get it checked out. It seems early for the
menopause to be calling in, but who said biology ever
respected norms and averages? Guess someone's got to be
on the tail of the distribution. I'm also seeking round for a
good counsellor. For me to see. You'll guess from that, how
horrible I've been. The acid test is, when I start damaging
those I love best, and I hope you know I mean you, then I'd
better look round for someone who'll help me stop doing
what I least want to do. But of course, for someone in my

trade, such things are never easy. I know most of the local practitioners, socially as well as professionally, especially any of the dyke practitioners ... and of course I want a sympathetic woman, not someone like that sleaze I foolishly spoke to earlier, who sees my love for a woman as 'The Problem'. Please! So it's not going to be easy for the therapist to find a therapist. I can hear Angus laughing about that already, but I'd rather make him laugh than you cry.

And about the agenda setting thing which you see happening between us. Have given it some thought. I know you suggested it mightn't be a high priority for me right now, but it is. You're important to me, always. Even when I've got the nail-gun out. And also, if I'm being really honest, maybe it's simpler to sort that one out than some of the other issues facing me. I think you might be copping some of my desire to be organising other people's lives. See, as a 'good-girl' therapist I have to refrain from telling my clients what they should do. Have to help them discover the solutions to their problems on their own. Mostly I manage this without sweat. But sometimes my mouth starts itching as if a truckload of ants had gotten in and bitten my tongue, I long to say, 'Why don't you ...?' especially when the answer seems obvious and they've been circling round it forever. But I restrain my burning tongue and say gentle, helpful, non-directive things ... but I'm wondering whether all this has a cost. Namely that when I leave the consulting rooms I feel 'off the leash', like I've earned the right to set agendas in all the other lives around me. Ever since this occurred to me, I've thought it was spot on. Guess seeing the problem is one thing, solving it will be harder. One step at a time, though.

Probably should sign off now, before I have any more deep 'revelations' about the bleeding obvious, or trot out another piece of pop psychology. What did I dump on you for? Thinking you were super-sophisticated because you'd 'discovered' some simple truth? And here I am doing the same. Mirror, mirror. God how I regret saying those things. I wince, knowing that I wrote them deliberately to hurt you. Not, I hasten to add, that I expect you to feel sorry for me.

Now, what would you like to write to me about in your next letter? There, have I avoided setting you an agenda? No, when I re-read that I realise, I'm still setting the agenda ... assuming that you will write to me again. This is going to be a hard habit to break, I can see. Anyway without any more navel-gazing, let me just say that I love you passionately. Hope I can become a better friend somehow (do they still make miracles?) and that you will write to me sometime about whatever you damn well please. I'll be puppy-pleased to get anything from you.

Love from Molly.

PS I did like the bed piece, a lot. Guess you'll dismiss that as pure suck and sycophant, but I'll say it anyway. It made me smile, sigh and climb appreciatively onto my bed, much to Ania's surprise, as I'm not usually one to go to bed at 11 am, unless I have a sore head or luscious lover in hand.

Dear Molly,

What a curious mea culpa letter that was. Am pleased that you are seeking out some support. And hope you find a person with robust shoulders, who'll help you surf through this turbulence. Not so sure about this HRT business, though. Have you talked to the doctor about options? It really worries me, and the feminist analysis, as you can imagine, is fairly critical of the "put the difficult old woman on a pill" mentality of many of the esteemed medical profession. Still, I'm sure you'll make wise choices. I know a lot of my women friends who've researched all the options, tried to engage positively their menopausal symptoms, read their Germaine Greer attentively, but found in the end, that HRT worked and they could then get on with whatever else they wanted to do without feeling either exhausted or incinerated. Have you been having those power surges, otherwise known as hot flushes? I gather they're quite extraordinary.

What's been happening up this way? I'll take that safe path as my rambling non-agenda. Well Lola is her usual self. Exuberant about everything, even her maths homework! A daughter can seem passing strange to a mother sometimes. She has a really intelligent teacher this year, one who actually takes pleasure in a questioning mind. Not like the rigid naysayer last year who thought her curiosity and desire for a bit more reading was a "problem"! Sometimes my pacifist philosophy is hard to sustain.

Anyway she's having a great year, starting to read chapter books all by herself and other such achievements. She has one friend at school that Angus and I instinctively dislike and distrust. Find ourselves discussing her in terms of her being a "bad influence". It can give you a shock, being a parent. But all the stories Lola brings home about this girl suggest that she's a manipulative exploiter, the kind who solicits confidences from soft kids like Lola and then broadcasts them to the mob for ridicule next day. But it's impossible, and perhaps not desirable, to try to influence the relationships your kids decide to cultivate, I guess. And I imagine it only escalates from here on. You didn't really talk about Leigh in your last letter, have there been any changes? Did she benefit from the visit to the health centre? And you know that all the offers I made in my ridiculously hippyish letter still stand. Though perhaps I'll make you up a bed, alone, in Lola's cubby house, if you want to visit but are still inclined to be savage.

Do you remember if your parents tried to influence you over your choice of friends at school? Think my mum liked most of the girls I brought home, all the dags who actually enjoyed classes. Later, she hated the fact that all the boys I dated were boneheads ... but then when I started going out with older, supposedly more sensitive, men, that's when things went badly wrong. That was in the years after you'd left school.

Anyway speaking of bad influences, had a long letter from my London lover the other day. She broke up with the whippetty one a few years ago and is now happily settled with a strong, companionate woman, and a cat, generally enjoying the comforts of living in a sunny cottage in a suburb where the original working-class inhabitants take open dykedom in their egalitarian stride. She's having an exhibition of her photographs next month, which was the excuse for the letter to me. Would love to see it but second semester will have started by then, so I can't. Was good to hear from her though, and I will try to see her, and her partner, next time I'm down that way.

Thought I'd enclose a couple of poems. If we're going to keep writing to one another, I guess I can't keep prattling on about Lola's school friends and the weather. Can't see that really being "us" ... whatever "us" might be after recent events? Guess I feel I need to try to re-establish a sense of trust in you. Though there are some stories I'll never be able to tell you. Be sure you don't "critique" these offerings when you're in the mood for burning. One is unashamedly hippy and celebratory. The other arose out of the turbulence we've recently experienced. Anyway, won't say any more, hope this finds you floating not thrashing.

Lots of love
Finn

Away with Espalier

there is a definite preference for the pared and spare and i know i can
do the thin and elegant and barbie likes it and so does a d hope
is there space for luscious profuse lush sprawling pumpkin vine fat strong rococo curls and
lots of tendrils lascivious repetitions
sensual sensuous sinuous phrases that wind around and around and round
your senses until you are dazed dizzy dreaming you are the poem and it is you
in a fertile smoke a tropico-humid haze of pleasing pleasurable sensations
as the words worlds tread finger lightly on your tender heatplump hips
or meet your lips like a mango daiquiri on a fresh baked december day
you remember your first pleasuring was it with you
or with a later lover who knew a little more about the bits that
needed kneading airbrushing finger flicking
or just good old-fashioned kissing
drift to an epiphany for the washing machine
its wondrous efficiency how it does what it says it will do every time you press
its sleek little buttons and beeps pertly when it's done and reliability is such
a rare rare commodity these days and for that you do
in a surprised kind of way love the white-goods you live with
the new fridge is up there too after so many years wrestling
kelvinators that needed weekly defrosts and out-of-balance twin-tubs that bucked
these solid fussless machines that wash and cool are not to be knocked
in an anti-suburban fashion frenzy which thinks it's hot to celebrate
the street-edge homeless and barbie begins to look jolly-hockey-stick healthy
in comparison to the starved anaemic girl/boys who feign death in the ads
i'll never find pallid shaking hunger attractive
no matter what it's supposed to be selling
give me the plump safety of this green patch any day
the trees grow and crop in urgent quiet
laved by carpet cool grass
which i mow as gladly as i comb my daughter's hair
knowing when i've finished i can see where i've been and for that i am grateful
so much of my life seems to have been a matter of breaking up
large cave-blocking rocks and carefully moving all the tiny pieces
to different locations only to realise that they needed moving again and so on and on and
there's never a sense of satisfaction even on a small scale
so i moor here in this brief haven just 50 perches and the pleasure of it
gives me an intense and tiny shock every now and then
like a fingernail on an up nipple and makes me globed and happy
even if i look thin and anxious and maybe that's why i move away from
all the training in espalier the tidy trimmed tied-up tree
against the wall
fruiting neat green pears with slender constraint
come close now to the big-hipped mango tree which lumbers birth squatting
in every tropical street and garden
demand-feeding off city water restrictions
drop-smashing fecund through greenhouse walls
fruit rot ferment lolling the lorikeets rainbow slow
greendark trees with magenta furbelows
make massive sky parlours where the chocolate skeins of satan velvet bats
cathedral their *canto diabolo*
the mango trees bear buxom luscious cupid-fruit
see the way they
toss the dense muscled flesh free sprawling into any lawns lap

The Kali in Me

the storm
assesses the city
for vulnerability

it's not the standard
poise-cool cotton thunderhead

this storm ferments
a core of twisting fumes
turbid canyons of cloud
cocked
    appraising
      vicious

its chain-mail
glinting sinister

it dresses the sky
in my storm logic

the Kali in me
riles alive
urgent as electricity
to drench and flood
split and spike

    this hard-won pastorale
    this milky tranquillity

July 25

Dear Finn

Thanks for the calm chatty letter, a kind of word-balm, I'm thinking. Perhaps having an aging hippy as a friend is not such a bad thing after all. Who else would be able to brew such a healing poultice out of minor news and a couple of poems? Took your advice. Yea! Don't die of shock! Read them in the comfortable hour following the eating of one of Ania's beetroot risottos, when it's extremely difficult, even for me, to feel anything but benign. Enjoyed the first poem a lot, though I think I'd get more out of it if I heard you read it to me. Maybe I will take you up on the offer of the cubby house retreat ... perhaps PRT would be more effective that HRT in treating whatever's wrong with me. Yes I rather fancy Poetry Reading Therapy over Hormone Replacement Therapy. Do you think it could take off? Imagine a large group of older women lying like sleepy dugongs on your back verandah as you plied them with poems and fresh lemongrass tea, lashings of your divine vegetarian lasagne, and platters of home-grown pawpaw. Reckon it'd cure most of their ills in a week, don't you?

The other poem was far more of a straight-in-the-vein hit for me. I knew exactly that feeling. Would you mind if I showed it to one of my clients? Feel it might release something in her, something which badly needs unlocking. If she could see another woman expressing savagery with calm-strong words which do no harm to anyone, maybe it would be some kind of swap for the destructive models she's experienced. See what faith I have in the power of your words? You really can trust me ... I think! And speaking of trust, what's with this 'I'm not telling' business? If there are things you want to keep secret, that's fine. But the mysterious hints are really annoying. I've been so clear about not setting you agendas lately, it's not fair of you to make out that I am. Is it? If you don't want to talk about whatever happened after I left school, just don't. I told you, my voracity and curiosity are under control. And I mean it.

Guess I should follow your lead and give you an update on the home front, given that I've been so busy nailing you to the wall that I've been forgetting to mention what's been happening. Well Ania has been just wonderful – calm, spacious, supportive, but at the same time not letting me get away with too much in the way of viciousness. I feel very lucky to have her around. I'm still discussing HRT and other options with the doctor, but haven't found a counsellor that I feel I can trust. So I've taken up long-distance lap-swimming instead. Ania bought me some bright yellow fins and some really up-market goggles. So I go up to the indoor pool (no weather-made excuses) every morning, and swim fiercely for an hour. Am doing three km now and feel heaps better, in every respect. Thought Leigh might enjoy it too but she's only come once and I'm not going to push it given the delicate truce we seem to have between us for the moment.

Find myself reluctant to put down words about this, even to you, or maybe it's me who can't be trusted. The GP that Leigh saw is brilliant. Intelligent, clear-headed and not judgmental. I'm so grateful for that. She hasn't prescribed lots of drugs or anything. They're trying out some homoeopathic drops, and Leigh sees her fortnightly for what sounds like an informal counselling session. I'm impressed with this as a treatment regime, and try desperately not to mentally strip-search Leigh when she gets back each time. It's really hard.

I imagine she spends the whole hour in there bad-mouthing me. Makes me want to scream out my defence, and parade my love for her as proof that I am a GOOD MOTHER. But I know I must hold tight, making it clear that I care, but equally that I respect Leigh's privacy. It's her right to completely malign me in front of a complete stranger. There I've said it. That's what I fear most, and feel most ashamed about fearing.

A couple of times, in those 3 a.m. sessions when my brain resembles a whirlpool with Attention Deficit Disorder, I've argued with myself about going to see this same doctor. She may be able to help me too, I argue. But if I put my head further under that load of toxic fairy-floss, I know that my stronger motivation is to see her so I can put my side of the case. At the very least to show her I'm not a vampiric, three-headed, daughter-mutilator. All this shows how paranoid and ridiculous I'm being. I don't even know that there's a case to answer. Whether Leigh has even blamed me once for any of her difficulties. Or whether, and this is a big blow to a mother's ego, she doesn't see me as central to her life at all right now, and maybe hasn't even mentioned me to the doctor. Can't decide which might be worse, that she says I'm the source of all evil, or the source of precisely nothing. Guess the latter would be better, when I write it out that way. I'm so ashamed about feeling this egocentric stuff, when a truly 'good' mother would simply be focused on getting her daughter well again. Guess the other side of mother blaming is just that, mothers feeling responsible for everything to the point of laughable self-importance. Now it's four o'clock but I feel so frazzled after writing that down, I think I need to do another 3 k.m. swim. The laps of the penitent, perhaps?

No, I can't write more. I've probably shown more of me than is tolerable in a world full of obscene egos. Hope you'll feel inclined to write to me again sometime, though I'll understand if you think I'm beneath contempt.

Love always – Molly.

PS After my swim I showed Ania this murky letter, and she said the only good thing in it was the tribute to the calming effects of her beetroot risotto. So she's including the recipe for it, hoping that Angus will cook it for you some time when you're feeling less than completely calm.

Beetroot Risotto

2 small fresh beetroot, with leaves still attached to stem
$2^1/2$ cups of good vegetable stock
1 tablespoon of olive oil
1 large Spanish onion, finely chopped
1 clove of garlic, finely chopped
200 g (1 cup) arborio rice
125 ml dry white wine
1 tablespoon of lemon juice
2 fresh basil leaves, finely chopped
25 g finely grated Parmesan cheese
Shaved Parmesan, extra

Remove beetroot leaves; wash well, chop roughly and set aside.

Cook whole beetroot in boiling water for 30 mins, or until tender. When cool enough to touch, peel them and then puree until smooth. (This is a very witchy looking mixture, which Leigh used to call bats' blood when she wasn't so sure about the benefits of having Ania in our lives.) Then put the bats' blood and stock in a suitable cauldron and bring to a simmer over medium heat.

In the meantime, heat olive oil in a large saucepan, add onion and garlic, cover and cook over very gentle heat for 8–10 minutes, stirring occasionally. Add rice, stir till all grains are coated with oil and toast lightly. Add wine and stir over high heat until liquid is absorbed. (The cook will definitely need a glass of wine to drink at this point.) Add 1 cup of the simmering bats' blood and stock mixture and stir over medium heat for 5 minutes or until all liquid is absorbed.

Add remaining mixture, half-a-cup at a time, stirring constantly, allowing each addition to be absorbed before adding the next. (This is the perfect time for Lola to brew an enormous tantrum, if she really wants to ruin the risotto and the evening!) Stir in lemon juice, basil, beetroot leaves, plus parmesan, and a bit of black pepper.

Serve in white bowls to really show off the extraordinary colour, scatter shaved Parmesan on top. A great full moon dish.

Dear Molly,

Say a huge thankyou to Ania for that amazing risotto recipe. As soon as I showed it to Angus he got all enthusiastic and took himself off to the shops to ferret out some fresh beetroot. He had so much fun cooking it that he leapt right out of his macrame-tight mood about having had a bad day at work and into his most benign and relaxed self. Beetroot magic! Lola enjoyed the bats' blood look, and I found the taste pretty fantastic too. So it was a success all round.

On to more serious matters. You sound as though you're wading barefoot through a particularly malodorous patch of the mangrove swamp, spiking your tender soles at every step on razor clam shells and those aerial roots which poke up out of the mud. After our recent skirmish, you will understand though, if I'm a bit shy about giving you any advice, though I do feel for you, and in true hippy-mother fashion, wish I could help somehow. The swimming sounds great though. Your leg muscles and pectorals must look fabulous!

Luckily for both of us, I have a lecture to write for tomorrow and have only just finished researching it, so really don't have time to dream up anything approaching simplistic advice. My understanding of the mother-daughter relationship is rather embryonic, and emerges mostly in my poems. So, I'll send you a couple on the topic and that will have to do for now. Maybe they'll prove therapeutic somehow. Maybe release something? If you hate them, could I suggest that you bin them, rather than dump on me? My skin is only just recovering from your last nail-gun adventure. I do have to rush, so will just stuff the poems in an envelope, how I miss you and wish I could do something really healing or soothing for you.

Love always
Finn

The Gift Arrives

'One day the gift arrives — outside your door'
Kevin Hart "The Gift"

did it then?
lucky you
sitting in your motorised recliner
electric doorbell chimes and
there it is
the gift
lavishly wrapped
of course
shiny sticky see-through
cellophane with ribbons
lustrous with luxury
not a cost in sight
this gift
just for you
no need
to worry   where it came from
             what strings
             what you need to do to keep it

my gift
came other wise
no simple ticket-gamble
an accident of dancing lust
and this gift
welded to my womb
space of ancient scars
twisting at the new
nurturing ask

season-long wrestling
with words and swamp-demons
brought us to clear-water
invisible intimacy months
then the swell to make us real to others

the gift inside
a tiny door — of sorts
centimetres small
the door that every time must stretch and burning stretch

well-known stranger
gift that gives such
strenuous learning curves
to the one who must
keep it
alive a love

a struggle so
the mother dreams open
the little bloody wrist-doors — centimetres small
to let her get some rest

the gift
so dancing potent
shifting not just the furniture
she shifts the bloody architecture
once let in/out/in

the gift
i see
a different way
a hundred times a day
    irrefusable
the one for whom my breasts made milk

no easy delivery
no luxury wrappings
except the ones i wove in plush-red-flesh
            o what a magnificent placenta!

but nonetheless

the gift

She's at School

Bring her back — now —
need to comb her skin
        breathe her hair
           anoint her scars
                teach her songs —
                  — no —
need to learn her songs ...

Like the one she sang at two, intent, wheeling in open space,
wheeling seer, dancing my black Bonds singlet like an opera queen,
singing deep, singing "I'm a big woman, I'm a big woman" —
attuned,
intense with power.

No — you can't have her
to chapel
to chastise
to cramp and to crimp
to tie to your Anglican-tight grids and graces.

She sings shouts into my belly
mouth pressed vibrant against my womb-walls,
her first home,
she's found this clever way back in,
her first haven,
singing laughing loud into my flesh
till her voice vibrations tingle me and
we fold into each other melding laughing.

Won't mention love, the word's so weak and worn,
        except to say
it creaks and ripples along our eight limbs
    articulate as bone
        smooth as sinew
           integral as 'e' & 'r' in mother daughter

August 25

Dear Finn

Was terrific to get your letter, even such a small one ...
I'm not complaining mind! And the poems made up for the
letter's brevity anyway. Dare I say anything about them,
given the tricky stuff we've just been through? I'll try, though
the nail-gun's in the garden shed – and I'm not. The one
about the daughter going to school brought on three
sodden hankies. I remember just that kind of intense
closeness between Leigh and I. That's what makes the vast
distance now between us so bloody hard. You think it'll
always be there, that joyous melding. You come to need it
like a drug, at least that's what I did. Then one day, the
supply gets cut, and going cold turkey on a daughter's love
is the pits.

As you might gather from this, life is still full of unlovely
contradictions. They're not the kind you can frolic in, more
like a huge series of swells and dumpers. I've cracked my
neck on the sand too many times to mention, my
swimmers are full of grit, my lungs feel bloated with water
and most days it's a struggle just to breathe. Ania is in full-
time lifesaver mode, which is wonderful and very
necessary. But I worry about the strain it puts on her, on
top of her complicated work. I'm still swimming a
desperate 3 k.m. every day, and I've decided two things.
One is to give up looking for a therapist. It's proving too
damn hard. The other is that I think I will start on HRT.
In most ways I don't want to. It's like you've got to take it
forever once you start it. The long-term effects are
unknown, but, and it's a pretty big but, I'm so close to
drowning and this seems the best life raft around. I don't
feel I can be too choosy. Is this making sense to you?
Perhaps not, it's very difficult to follow my logic at present,

even for me, and I'm inside my head. Most days I wish I wasn't.

Leigh is a bit easier to be with. At least she's stopped pissing in the jar in her room. And she hasn't stopped seeing that doctor at the Women's Health Centre. I'm so grateful for that. So I guess outsiders would say things are more stable, and I can see that they are. But I'm still feeling so much fear. Can only see this cool calm as temporary. Find myself checking the knife-block every night before I go to bed, in case she's taken one into her room, and keeping an accountant's eye on all the pills, from the painkillers to the decongestants. She isn't so elaborate about avoiding me at present but when I go to hug her, it's like getting intimate with a suit of chain mail. I'm allowed to touch the shell, the metal-hard exterior, but as for those once normal, total meldings, which you so accurately describe, forget it. And I bloody miss them.

You know how when the placenta detaches, there's that really big open wound inside and you bleed for about six weeks? Well that's how I feel right now. This huge bit of my life as a mother has been 'untimely ripped'. I'm powerless to stitch it back. It's taking such a long time to heal ... most times I can't see that it ever will. Every time I see Leigh adopt a kind of armoured posture as I approach, every time I attempt a silly joke with her and it bounces off the armour with a tinny clunk, the wound re-opens and I bleed inside and it just won't stop. Am I being too melodramatic? How do other mothers live through this?

Maybe I should come up to you for a visit, you're the only one I know who'd understand the feelings and may be able to help me get them sorted. Is there any time in the near future when a visit from a drowning woman wouldn't be a horrific inconvenience to you, Angus and Lola? Let me know what you think. I'll understand completely if it can't work. I was twisting myself up, not even wanting to ask, but Ania said to just do it. Let you decide what is and isn't possible for you. So I trust that if you want to say no, for even the slightest reason, and I can't imagine why you'd want to say yes, that you would. Have just re-read that sentence and see how hopeless it is, but I probably couldn't improve on it in my current state of mind so it'll just have to stay that way. Knowing you, I'm sure you'll be able to work out what it means.

On to other matters. We're pretty close to deciding to go to that school re-union. Do you remember me mentioning it a few months ago? Ania is mobilised on it. I think she's kind of hoping that a change of scene and something else to think about might help. Also we both think that four days here on her own might be useful to Leigh, a chance to prove her independence and enjoy it without me hovering about. I'm still not sure. Just writing about it fills me with panic. Not sure if I can do this, given my sense of the uncertainty of just about everything. What do you think?

Will finish this now. It's the kind of letter I hate to write. I feel ashamed of, but also better for, writing it, if you can follow that. Please write soon, I miss you, and you can write about anything, just please write.

Love – Molly.

Dear Molly,

Well I was glad you wrote to tell me how you really are, but very sorry that you are so really at sea. Could you ring the doctor who's caring for Leigh and discuss your situation briefly? See if she knows anyone you can get help from? She may be linked into completely different networks to the ones you know and be able to come at the problem from a fresh angle. Would be worth a try if you can face the effort. Of course you might ask Leigh about it first, so she doesn't think you're slyly encroaching on her territory. It's so wonderful that she's still seeing the doctor. You don't want to jeopardise that.

As for the school re-union ... why not try it? It's only four days, and it may do you all good to have a complete break from the normal routines and have a breather. (Is that another homespun cliche? Too bad, I'm just going to persevere, or I'll never be able to write more than five lines to you!) Maybe part of the issue is to do with the role of lifesaver. That's what mothers are expected to be, isn't it? To act as stalwart, rescuer, the one who's always there, stable and reliable in any emergency ... but maybe Leigh is saying that at 17 she can quite capably swim on her own, get herself into difficulties, and get out of them too. After all, you've spent a huge amount of energy teaching her how to swim and how to rescue herself. Maybe she wants to be allowed to try those skills out on her own and let you have a rest? So maybe, just maybe, you could think of the four days as time for the lifeguard to go off-duty and have some fun after being swamped by all those dumpers? The equivalent to a few days on a Li-Lo on a lake? Is this resonating anywhere in your weary body? After all, it's not as if you were planning six weeks away in the Tanami Desert out of phone range. And didn't you buy Leigh a mobile phone a little while back so she could always contact you? Of course I know it wouldn't be easy leaving her, but it sounds as though staying isn't all that easy either.

As I write all this I feel a little anxious, as I always do when giving advice. It's a strange practice isn't it? I know you struggle with not appearing to give advice to your clients, which must be a bit like trying to muster fleas. Is that an accurate description? And in my job it's a surprisingly common requirement. When I'm supervising students' projects, there's an implicit obligation for me to advise them on issues. I find it a real challenge. Because even though both parties know it's expected, and even desired by the student a lot of the time, there's still the awkward business of the giving, and the taking in, of the suggestions. And then the shark-fins of doubt start nosing around: what if the advice is off-beam, inappropriate, too much, too little, too bossy, too gentle, too distant, too personal? It's a subtle and tricky business, isn't it? And I've been the recipient of some horribly wrong advice. And then had to live with the consequences of following it. Whereas the advice-giver has gotten off without a single draughty chink of doubt in their smugness.

Suppose I'm also especially sensitive about giving you advice because of our recent difficulties. If I suggest that you go away, and then things go wrong, will that add to the tensions between us? Maybe even end the friendship? But I guess you did ask me what I thought, and I'm incapable of sitting on my banana lounge by the pool impassively sipping mango daiquiris when someone I love is floundering. I'd always rather be passionate and wrong than sit minimal and safe on some fence. Fence sitting seems downright dangerous to me, doesn't matter what kind of fence you choose. There's always going to be some danger to your posterior I figure, so you might as well take the risks involved in jumping to one side or the other, or in my case, jumping backwards and forwards energetically whenever I please. I admit I've had a few nasty snags over the years from this (f)risky practice, but that's better than getting splinters in your buttocks, or having barbed wire rake the length of your tender inner thigh.

Suppose while we're on the topic of boundary bounding ... it might be a worthwhile distraction for me to tell you what happened next in that saga you asked me to embark on some months ago. Well, I didn't see Ms Luscious of London for quite a while after that humiliating lunch. Every couple of years we would bump into each other at a market or party, or send a postcard or somesuch. In that desultory kind of way we kept in touch, both interested to know what the other was doing but not with any yearning unresolved lust. Humiliation has never been a factor in provoking or sustaining erotic desire for me. And you? Maybe all those years of being taken under the house by the neighbour and having him do humiliating and excruciating things to my body, cured me of any of the masochistic desire some psychoanalysts say is a "natural" part of the female psyche. What a convenient thing to believe, that those with less power enjoy a bit of pain and suffering! Anyway, maybe I'm unnatural but pain and abasement just don't do it for me.

So Ms Luscious settled into a more consistent lifestyle with her friend, and Angus and I met up. I still wasn't sure what the London episode meant about my sexual identity but there was something flickering fish-fast between him and me, so I just jumped gleefully over the fence again and enjoyed it. And as we were both fit and young, and keen as beach balls on a windy day, it was worth quite a bit. I've dug out this poem I wrote about that time ... not sure that you'll love it but once upon a time you did say you were interested.

Lips

two lovers
pressing
lightly together
two lips
smoothing sweeps of skin

two lips conversing
moving more
conversation sensation
becoming
pressing pleasure

a pause
he seeks
again
the secret talk
of her other mouth
longing
to be wrapped in
her rich & subtle
he wants
not to penetrate
he seeks
entrance

two lips
warm smooth slide speak yes
speak   entrance

It's not one of my favourites and I must say it feels a bit odd sending that particular one to an all-her-life lesbian, but maybe it can explain some of the differences?

Doing the "smooth slide speak yes" and taking Angus within my muscular "other mouth" makes me feel both powerful and cherished. There's huge satisfaction in knowing my body carries the power to gratify him. He, and other men whom I've "entranced"(!), seem to feel so humbly grateful for the way my muscles and that glorious spontaneous mucous can enfold, grip and wrap them into the rhythms of rapture. Afterwards I feel sated, but also somewhat queenly. And that kind of power, generated between two close bodies, neither one dominated by the other, but feeling equal and creative, able to merge so thoroughly and then to separate into a state of being calmly independent, that's the kind of power I desire and admire most profoundly.

There I've gone and got all lyrical about sex, and it's not even lunchtime. Writing to you does odd things to me! I'll have to wash my face carefully before I head off to give that lecture on Working Conditions in Eighteenth Century Britain.

I was really glad you asked about coming up to visit ... you might remember I suggested it several letters ago (she says with a wry smile). Anyway, we've discussed it and we'd all dearly love to see you. Dates are a bit unclear because Angus has to go away a couple of times over the next few months and Lola has a school camp. At present I'm trying to muster all the dates for these events and then I can call you with a few suggestions. We might, be still my beating heart, even be able to get away for a few days alone on The Island. How I would love to lie you down on one of those gently sloping, clear-of-people beaches and administer the very best in swimming and relaxation therapy. So, I'll be in touch soon about times. Until then, remember to drift towards the Li-Lo and the lake, instead of eternally lumbering on as lifeguard.

Also remember — I love you —
Always — Finn

September 20

Dear Finn

Was great to get your letter and see that you're willing to follow the agenda I set back in January, was it? Actually it did me a lot of good, gave me a sense of the continuity of my interests or life or something. The poem and following discussion were intriguing, if a bit confronting to someone who has never done 'It' with a man. Asking that gay friend of Audrey's to wank into a jar when we wanted his sperm for the inseminations which were to lead to Leigh's conception, was hardly erotic. And neither was the turkey baster we used to get the semen into the right place! It was all terribly ideological and serious. Felt medicinal more than anything, all of a piece with the strict feminist separatist position we held in the 1970s, but erotic, never. Certainly nothing like the pleasure you so indecently describe. You're right, the power dynamics of sex are every bit as interesting as the sensual bits. Well, perhaps not every bit, but they are worth looking at when there isn't a lover around to actually do things with! But there's this ridiculous imperative to be polite, to never mention the sometimes fierce urge for power (both creative as well as destructive) we all experience, but mustn't ever admit to in public. But I must say when Ania is lying there looking beatific after one of our sessions, like you, I feel an intense satisfaction and sense of my own power, knowing that I'm able to navigate her passions. It's like white-water rafting, being both sure and unsure about my ability to steer her to calm bliss at the end of each wild ride.

Enough on sex, that's not all there is in life, after all. Know what you mean about the giving of advice. Sometimes when I feel particularly tense about it, I decide I'll never give another bit of it as long as I live. But then someone comes mourning round and I can't help myself. Suddenly I find myself making helpful suggestions again. Perhaps it's the eternal lifeguard syndrome, or maybe it's because I've made a zillion mistakes and now know some strategies that help to soften the hurts. Or do you think I could be addicted to playing the wise woman dispensing wisdom to all who come seeking? Because you're right, there is frequently a push — professional or otherwise — to give advice and it seems unworthy to avoid that just because it makes you a bit anxious.

And I did ask for your advice about several things in my last letter ... and don't die of shock ... I'm actually going to heed it. Firstly, I talked to Leigh about me ringing her doctor and she said she really didn't mind. So I did and we had a deep chat. She sounded salty and sensible and didn't show a flicker of mother-blame. And I know I'd have picked it up if there'd been any around. Said she understood completely how I might be feeling. Gave me the name of a woman counsellor, of whom I know NOTHING, and I'm going to see her next week.

Then Ania and I discussed the re-union and decided we would actually go. Gulp! Put it to Leigh and she said she'd be fine, might invite one of her close friends over for part of the time. I was so relieved, I wanted to crush her unblemished face to my unruly chest. I had thought a friend to keep her company would be a neat solution to my anxieties but hadn't wanted to make helpful suggestions, or appear over-protective. We've decided to make it a more leisurely break and do the reunion but also just have a few quiet days around the edges. Hopefully I can make a jug of mango daiquiris or something equivalent for Ania. I'd like to give her some cosseting after all the recent turmoil.

Have also decided to put off embarking on HRT for the moment. The reunion is the week after next, so I thought I'd see how the break went. Then see if the counsellor helped. And depending on when I can come up to see you, maybe even put it off until after that visit. Then I'll take stock and see if I really need to take the 'difficult old lady cure' that the pharmaceutical companies are making so much money out of.

By the way, how did your Eighteenth Century lecture go after all those unseemly thoughts? And how is the date mustering going, anything firming up yet? Do let me know. Ania is taking a week off to do the reunion thing so she probably won't be able to get away again in order to come up north. I think she secretly loves the thought of having some time alone without my opera-queen act. She'd never say it, but I think she's a bit sick of me singing loud tragic arias through all her days and nights!

Hoping to hear from you soon – love from Molly.

Dear Molly,

It's always good to hear from you, but your last letter was especially welcome because it had some of your old sting in it. Never thought I'd want to hear your Commandant Icebloch voice again but after the past few anaemic months, I love hearing you being bossy and setting agendas. Amazing.

Before I wander on to anything else, I've finally mustered all the dates of happenings here and it looks like there's a clear gap round the end of this month, right up to about the middle of November. How would that fit for you? When does Leigh sit her HSC exams, aren't they in November sometime? Anyway, let me know and I'll start ironing the sheets and baking your favourite biscuits ... well at least getting in a good supply of the beer you like best!

Lola has been crook this week, and of course it happens in a heavy week of lectures, one of those weeks where I'm doing several guest spots in other people's courses on top of the usual load and, wouldn't you know it, Angus is frantically preparing a major report for a big meeting he's going to in Canberra on Thursday and Friday. We both look like undernourished raccoons with the strain of staying awake through several sleep-raddled nights, and biting each other on the tender bits out of sheer tiredness. Some days the effort of going to work and looking normal is just enormous. How have you managed with your clients over the past turmoily months? When I meet mothers with three or four kids plus full-time work I reach in my pocket for a Bravery and Sheer Amazement Award. How do they manage? There's one woman, she's got a kid in Lola's class (plus three younger ones), and she manages to look cheerful and to wear white linen suits ... must be a different breed to the slapdash stock I come from.

Anyway poor old Lola has a bad dose of giardia, and has been off school for the past three days ... doesn't feel like eating and has no energy. Such a contrast to her usual sea-constancy. In exasperation Angus said, "She couldn't have picked a worse time to get sick" ... well did that raise my maternal tigress! I pointed out that she didn't choose to get an infestation of parasitic protozoa in her stomach, so "pick" was a totally inappropriate term ... and that with the current increase in pressures we're both experiencing at work there was never a "better" time for her to get sick ... and she was only a little kid after all, and little kids have to get sick sometimes! We don't get frost up this way, as you know, but the air in the car was singing with ice particles after that sweet exchange. It's times like this that I long for a dream-mother who simply adores spending time with Lola, is her own independent woman, but has no pressing commitments in her life so that when we hit a nauseous patch like this, she could cheerfully and unresentfully look after Lola during the day, and then we'd come home to a house cinnamon-scented with baking, a well-loved child and a fulfilled nurturer. I'm pretty good at utter fantasy aren't I? But there must be a better way than this wading through half-set concrete, feeling that you're failing both at home and at work. I just want to spend the days on the bed with Lola, lying close as earth and rock, using all my will and love to heal her and help her endure the noxious medicine needed to knock off these particular greeblies. But I have this simultaneous desire not to stint on my work commitments ... aaargh ... it's too hard for me to conjure anything remotely resembling a solution, especially as it's 10.40 p.m., I'm supposed to be writing a lecture for tomorrow, and Lola will probably wake at least three times in the night. As Adele Horin says, it's "an untold epic ... only Odysseus himself wrestled ... so many monsters, fought so many battles, and endured such harassment as the average working mother encounters on her daily odyssey from bed to desk".

In spite of all that, I had to give in to the profligate desire to talk to you, it just helps to know you're there. Wrote a poem about your phone calls after the last one — you have to be the first to see it. I'll pop a copy in the envelope. Hope things are going smoothly in the preparations for your break, and am dying to hear how your session with the counsellor went.

> Even when I'm exhausted I love you
> Finn

It's You

phone demands
          again
at the fag-end of this endless day
      i clump angrily through the tired house
         answer it   and
                        it's you
you cool shower on a day that's just too hot
voice as loving as a finger-stroke on my bone-thin cheek
laughter as strong as my mother's hands
tender as the inside of my upper arm
so glad
        it's you

October 12

Dear Finn

Do ya like the postcard? Picked it specially, just for you!
Who would ever think of putting the power station at
sunset on a postcard? Crazy, but for some reason it made
me think of you. The leave-taking with Leigh went
smoothly, I didn't howl until we'd gotten round the first
corner. Ania just kept driving as I sobbed and demanded to
be taken back. Which was of course the best thing to do –
to just keep going. Since then Leigh has sounded
competent and even cheerful on the phone. Daughters and
their independence! I celebrate it with both hands but my
heart is quite another matter. Knew one postcard would
never be enough. I'll get some paper and sprawl.

A little later, after scratching madly round all the bags and
boxes, cursing loudly until I finally found the writing pad
which I'd packed in a 'safe' place ...

It's been good to get away. Before we left I took time to
research good eating places on our route north. So I've
been able to take Ania out to eat some great food ...
prawns nestling on beds of noodles and greens,
passionfruit bavarois, mango and chicken salad, and other
such delights. It's been a good cure for both of us. Also it's
been good to drive long-distance together. Don't you find
you have the most interesting in-depth talks like that?
Maybe it's because you feel cocooned in the car, or there
aren't any of the usual interruptions, or perhaps you're a
little looser than usual because you're on holiday, or maybe
it's being in transition so you get free of your everyday self.
Or a happy combination of all those things. Anyway we've
been nattering as we drive, enjoying each other's company
in a way we haven't had the space to do for ages. In spite

of the weather being a bit damp, we've stopped off for swims often and with all this we're sleeping wonderfully.

Know you hesitated about giving me advice about this trip but so far it has been great. So I owe you a huge thank you for getting off your banana lounge and risking it. Your gentle but firm brown hand in the small of my back was just what I needed to get me out of the doldrums. Have you seen that Judy Horacek cartoon about the woman in the rut? Ania packed a book of Horacek cartoons for our holiday reading and we've been enjoying them heaps. If I can find a photocopy place before I post this, I'll pop in a copy. Anyway, what I want to say is thank you for being such a strong friend, and helping me clamber out of that last gritty rut.

Tomorrow is the big reunion barbecue, only ex-students to attend. The next day there's a smorgasbord luncheon at the RSL (!) for all the reunionists plus partners and kids. Sounds bloody horrible to me but Ania reckons it'll be fascinating. Can't quite believe I'm doing this, feel curiously nervous as well as extremely curious. Ania reckons the pleasure of looking over the others will far outweigh the horror. Not sure that I agree ... they weren't all witness to her nightmare school days, were they? Anyway, I've come this far, so I guess I'll go ... wish me luck.

Till next time – love Molly.

UNREQUITED LOVE No. 35
It's not a rut
I'm just having a little rest
It's not a rut
horacek

October 14

Dear Finn

Well what an experience! It was so weird to see all those faces and bodies which were teenage last time you looked and are now a bit past forty. Joe Kirkham, you remember him, the footballer with the head like a Queensland Blue pumpkin? The one who got fewer marks in his HSC exams the second time he sat them? Well he'd really put on some plush, his face was as puce as a dog's dick. Soon as I arrived at the barbecue he came over and gave me this huge meaty hug, felt like I was being swallowed by a sausage machine. Ugh! Anyway we were exchanging niceties about what we'd done for the past twenty-five years, my smile just about to slide off my sweating face, when Harriet came up. She and I were pretty good friends the last two years at school, and we've kept in touch on and off since then. She came galloping over and immediately asked me how Ania was, were we still together? Joe was quietly busy with his beer, trying to suss out the implications of what was being said, and then asked me straight out, 'So, you living with a woman?' When I confirmed his worst suspicions he shook his head like a dog with water in its ears. 'Can't believe it. You, turning out lezzo. You know, I really fancied you back then. True life, you went in to box for the other side?' He shut up tight for a bit, while Harriet and I talked, then he said, 'I should've taken you out to the drive-in like I wanted to. Maybe you wouldn't have gone queer then, huh?' Can you believe it? I couldn't for a minute, but then I said with a light laugh, 'In your dreams, Joe' and he lumbered off to get another beer.

At that point I was just about ready to skip the rest and go home for an afternoon's musing on the bed with the beautiful Ania, but Harriet talked me into staying, and it did get better. Caught up with lots of the girls who'd been in the school swim team with me, and you and Ania were both right, it was pretty fascinating. I was the only out dyke there, though I have my inklings about some of the other women who passed themselves off as independent and single. You can't blame them I guess, it's still a pretty small town and lots of them have their parents and grandparents living in the district. Could put a bit of a downer on grooving along in an out lifestyle, I guess. I was surprised at the number of people who'd stayed round the district. Even those who'd gone on to uni, a lot of them had worked it so that they got positions back home. Funny, isn't it? That thought never occurred to me. I was so clearly focused on escaping, and even though I still love the landscape, I can't imagine striving to come back. Maybe the fact that Ruby and Bill moved to Brisbane two years into my degree made a difference, but I'm not sure. Think Ruby and I were both pretty locked into the driving necessity for escape from small-town, country thinking, that I should travel the globe in search of something more sophisticated. It's not how I'd see it now, but back then that was the goal for a 'bright girl with prospects'.

Anyway, the afternoon passed peaceably enough. Joe didn't come back to chat, though I saw him gossiping pretty intensely with some of the lads, casting sideways glances in my direction. I was sorry to upset his equilibrium! But I actually have to admit to enjoying myself. It was a big gossip all round really. So much hysterical reminiscing about stupid stuff that happened at school. Some of it I'd forgotten completely, but given a few beers and a few reminders, all the pranks and teachers' idiosyncrasies came back. It's always satisfying, crying with laughter ... and at the table I was sitting at we did plenty. So I got home to Ania about five in the evening, having sworn I'd only stay for a couple of hours. Was sporting a tear-stained face, but felt the very opposite of miserable. Ania was relieved to see me so relaxed. On the strength of that we went out dancing at one of the clubs. A few eyebrows got raised as we were obviously an item, and not in the least interested in the local boy talent. But to my huge relief no one felt obliged to hassle us, so we came home feeling like old puppets. You know those ones, with the floppy joint-strings?

Today was a bit of an anticlimax. Ania and I fronted up to the all-in-together get together but we didn't stay very long. The Normality Meter was primed and ticking. Competitive eyes, avid as currawongs', checking out partners and kids. Who'd done best – that's the game. One bloke went into a big rave to us about the jewellery being worn by another bloke's wife – the income barometer. This stuff I could miss. Kids paraded like pets at a pet show. No-one able to finish a story about their Nicole's achievements in ballet without being barrelled over by someone else boasting about their little Justin's achievements in computing. Bloody ghastly.

Ania and I had dressed in our dykish best, and were looking pretty sharp. We were the smartest-looking couple there, but after an hour or so, we both found the staring and not-so-subtle whispering directed at us, fairly wearing. One guy, do you remember him, Glenn Stoltenberg? Well he'd brought his male partner along, for which I felt immensely grateful. At his suggestion, the four of us grabbed a table as far away from the smorgasbord frenzy as possible and sat together making sharp comments about the passing parade. I didn't have much to do with Glenn when we were at school, but he proved to be terrific company, particularly in a situation like that. After about two hours I collected addresses from a couple of women, thanked the organisers of the whole shebang, blew Joe Kirkham a kiss, and loped off with Ania for a very long surf.

We'll start heading for home tomorrow morning early. So far all seems well with Leigh. Ella's visit went smoothly apparently, but you can imagine how keen I am to get back and see with my own hungry eyes. Will call you when we get there –

Lots of love – Molly.

October 18

Dear Finn

Was so good to get home. Everything was steady and calm
when we got back. There was a busload of washing and
washing-up lying around but apart from that Leigh had
managed well. Given my grisly nightmares about what
I might find lying or dangling around, dirty clothes and
dishes seemed a relief. She actually seemed pleased to see
her daggy old mother – gave me a real hug, left the suit of
armour off! You can imagine what that meant. I've even
been persuaded that she and Ella did some effective exam
preparation together.

And your letter was waiting here for me. So sorry to hear
about Lola's gut thing, is she over it now? And poor you,
sleep deprivation is terrible, isn't it? It seems so ordinary, it's
not easy for people to sympathise about, yet it's so
dangerous. I often wonder how many road accidents are
caused by parents suffering from a simple lack of sleep.
Do take care of yourself. Am I sounding too much like
Commandant Icebloch crossed with Mother McCredie?
Sorry.

About travelling north ... Leigh finishes her exams early in
November. So, she and I are talking about flying up to you
for a tropical post-exam treat. How would that suit? Would
Angus be home that week, 8th–16th? I was pretty hesitant
about suggesting it to Leigh, but when I mentioned it
obliquely she put her arms round my waist and said, 'Hey,
it'd be great to spend some time together, without any
pressure!' Said she knew what a tough year it'd been for
me. I found it hard to see the glass I happened to be
washing up at that moment. Finished the dishes and went
into the study for a quiet howl. I'm not sure that even you
can understand the huge relief it is to be allowed to be

close to Leigh again. Maybe the placenta-sized wound can heal after all. I'm not foolish enough to think we'll ever return to the closeness you and Lola have at present, but at least if the armour's off I can start to build a different relationship with this woman-daughter.

Didn't mention in my earlier letters the long talk I had with Dave Azzopardi when I was at the reunion. You know his older brother, Ed, drove his car full speed into a tree, deliberately, a few years ago? I think I told you about it. Well Dave and I had a really long yarn about it and how he's coped since then. Those brothers were so close. It seems Ed wanted to marry an Ozzie woman, a strong and loving companion according to Dave. But she was divorced and their old man forbade the marriage. He said he'd shoot her if Ed tried to bring any divorcee slut home. So Ed split up with the woman, said he didn't want to live in sin. He got a job on some really remote cattle property, and tried to forget all about her, but couldn't. Dave says he became quite obsessive and kept ringing her up late at night asking weird stuff about her ex and other stuff from her past, so finally she moved, leaving no forwarding address. Dave says this drove Ed frantic as he didn't want to lose her, but when he realised it was all over, he just lost it and a few weeks later killed himself. Dave blames his dad for the whole mess and wouldn't go home to the farm at all until his father died, not even to help with the harvest. So the poor mother is left on the farm, and they're trying to find a manager to run it. Dave has a job at the local agricultural station, which he loves, and he goes home on weekends to help out, as do both the girls who live nearby. You remember Giovanna, don't you?

Such a horrible thing, after all those years when they worked like ants to build that farm in the New Country, always with a view to creating a secure rural haven away from all the strife back home ... and now this mess. It's hard for Dave and his sisters, so tough picking through all the rigid expectations, like swimming through barbed wire. But it's the mother I feel for most. She adored Edoardo, her first-born son, and he was pretty gorgeous, powerful yet gentle. Do you remember him singing in the school musicals? And what must she have felt, as the father gave out his decrees and drove Ed away from home, following their Church's teaching to the letter, but at the same time destroying the family and all that she'd slogged to realise? And now she's left, like a beached whale, worn out and exhausted in that vast farm clearing, with only complicated memories for company. Can only hope her faith lives up to its claims of profound solace. Imagine she'd need every ounce of it to keep her going. Dave was very open, not ashamed to admit his pit of sadness about the whole thing. Says his father had horrific experiences during the war, which is one of the reasons why he was so keen to come to Australia, but some of the horror obviously wouldn't stay tidily behind – and now this. Don't think Dave will ever forgive his dad for, as he sees it, destroying Ed, and that's a pretty big burden to bear too. The aftermath and inter-generational effects of violence are so vast, aren't they? After the heroes come home, society seems to think it's all over. Convenient ... but so far from the truth.

As you can imagine, this talk had some (!) effect on me. Brought home yet again the effect of suicide on those left behind. Really not sure I could survive if Leigh ... no I can't even write it. Probably shouldn't have told you that story about the Azzopardi family, except I know you were friends with Giovanna. Have you kept in touch with her? And Dave asked closely after you, wanted to know if you'd gotten over your troubles. Didn't quite know what he meant, but gave him a quick account of what you're doing. Down, curiosity, down!

I'd best away, my client has arrived early. They're always a little unsettled when I've been away for a bit, so I'd best stop this profligate chatting (I love that phrase) to you, and put my professional face on. Hope to hear from you soon about our tropical holiday –

Lots of love – Molly.

Dear Molly,

What a feast of letters from you. I felt so indulged,
wallowing in your words. The reunion sounds amazing.
So Kirkham is still a bit of a jerk, eh? Some of the other bits
sound fun, and I felt immensely pleased to hear that it was
restorative. I rang Leigh while you were away, didn't ask
any probing questions, just chatted to her like an off-the-
leash aunt, and promised to make her mango daiquiris
next time she comes up, now she's come of age. Looks
like I may have to keep that promise soon! Can't quite
believe that you may both be up here in less than a
fortnight. It's fine with Angus and Lola. I won't have any
classes on then, as it's study vacation. May still have some
essays to mark but that's easy to work around. So make
the bookings, buy the tickets and start packing. And you
can believe that I'll start preparations at this end. So don't
change your mind!

Glad you told me about what happened with the
Azzopardis. Had heard about Ed's suicide but none of the
whys. I remember tales of his father warning people off
the property with a shot-gun even when we were at
school, and my mum saying how lonely Mrs Azzopardi
was because Mr A. was so paranoid he didn't like anyone
to visit. As you say, you can move countries and feel like
you've left everything behind, but the stuff you carry in
your head is harder to abandon. What you said about war
and its long-term impacts resonated with me, in that
strange deep way that happens so often between us. It ties
in with a poem I wrote a few months ago. I didn't send it
to you then, as it's not one that lightens your mood and at
that stage you were struggling to stay buoyant. But I'll
enclose it now, and get back to marking essays with an
added sense of urgency, knowing that if I get them done

quickly I'll be able to enjoy your visit unfettered by a sense of duty and guilt. A great incentive.

Did you catch up with Giovanna when you were at the reunion? Haven't heard any news from her for a couple of years now. She used to send cards every now and then. Also have a 25-watt memory that she once told me about an incident concerning a school billet and having to share a bed with you. Is that right? Funny I've never heard the tale from you, yet you keep pushing me to be open about my past ... hint, hint. Was kind of Dave to ask after me, and thanks for filling him in on what's been happening. Wouldn't mind getting his address from you sometime. He and Giovanna were very sweet to me when I most needed friends.

Tell Leigh, good luck and clear thinking in all her exams, and I'm really looking forward to celebrating the end of school with her! Sounds like the perfect excuse for some woman-sized wild nights. Let me know flight numbers and times as soon as you have them. Lola is busy painting a welcome sign and Angus is scuffling through his recipe books in search of the choicest dishes for your arrival feast. Can't wait till then, but I guess I'll have to.

Love you
Finn

First Wound

Want to know when I went?
Must have been 1915.
Nothing but mum's kiss on my face,
    and such smooth white skin,
        they reckon it was heaven sent.

Went straight to the front.
Knew bugger all about nothing.
All I wanted was sleep and
one of mum's square meals and
a game a cricket.
Yeah, mucking round with a ball in the backyard,
that's all I dreamt about.

Then I got hit,
bit of shell ripped into my arm.
Had a great set of biceps back then,
    smooth, strong, white,
        not these tawny chook's legs.
Bit of shell slashed right into the left one,
give me this bloody great gash.

Hurt? Yeah, it hurt, too right,
but it was the look of it that got me —
my smooth skin — suddenly ripped.

The orderlies were ready to brain me,
couldn't leave the dressings alone,
kept ripping them off to look, kept having to have a look.
My skin was white — clean — hairless —
not this pulpy mess.
Couldn't be me,
couldn't bear it being on me.
Wash it off. I said. Wash it off.
The orderlies had to strap me to the stretcher,
keep me from going at the buckets of water all the time.
Wash it off. I said. Wash it off.

Got over it,
came home with a jinkerful of medals.
Glad to get back with only a couple a' scars.
Then Edie come along,
we married,
and the babies came pretty soon after.
It was the thing to do.
All the blokes got into the wife and kids bit,
double quick,
wanting to get back to something normal.

Still had a bit of a thing about that first wound.
Washing the babies brought the memories back.
Why'd she have to have two girls —
        with their clean, white, hairless things?
Would've been different if Edie would've had some boys.
Why should they stay white and clean?

Bastards hadn't let me stay that way.
Can see it, can't you?
Had to make them red and pulpy,
        same as me.

So that's how it started.
I kept at them.
Like when I was first hit,
ripping at my dressings,
except there were no orderlies to stop me.
Edie tried a couple of times,
but I soon shut her up.
You learn a lot at the front.

Then my girls were gone —
made sure they never said anything,
no fear of that —
I started looking out for others.
pretty easy.
Pick out the busy mothers,
only too happy to have a break from the kids,
leave them with the war hero.

How many?
Don't know.
It's been so long.
Don't remember any of them specially.
Except my own girls,
they were my first.
They all look the same down there,
remind me of that bloody great gash they done to me ...
my smooth skin —

      suddenly ripped —
            couldn't bear it,
                 not me,
                 not this bloody mess.

November 1

Dear Finn

Just a quick one which should reach you before I do.
What a poem! I'm looking forward to talking it over with
you when I come up. Couldn't understand why you were
writing in the digger's voice, doing such a sympathetic
portrait and then it turns, and ugh ... gave me a bad case
of chicken skin. How do you come up with such things?
Have you sent it off for publication yet? Guess the RSL
Weekly wouldn't be the first place you'd try, right!?

Leigh is in the midst of her final exams and we're all trying
hard to stay calm in amongst all the hype. There are so
many myths about these Last Days deciding your Entire
Life ... I hate it. Sure it might have an influence, and in
some cases it is decisive, but none of it's forever. But there's
a kind of mass hysteria about, like a cloud of mosquitoes,
which is hard to escape. Still, I've felt proud of Leigh, she's
been extremely focused and the very opposite of
hysterical. She's kept going to see that GP, even though she's
been strapped for preparation time.

Feel so hugely grateful to this woman for her generous
healing. Yet I'm not sure how to tell her. I know we've both
had the same experience, where one of our clients or
students feel inordinately grateful to us for some help we've
been able to give, but we just see it as part of doing our
normal job. And another thing, there's a lot of guff in the
media about how we're failing our young people and
much quoting of the youth suicide rates, but where are the
research projects which record and analyse the kind of
preventative work that doctors like this one are doing? If
Leigh hadn't seen this woman, maybe she'd have been one
of those appalling statistics. Everyone is so much more
interested in the drama of failure than in the quiet joy of

success and gentle rescue. The way I feel, this woman should be front-page news for the subtle way she's nurtured Leigh. Suppose all I can do though, is send a carefully worded card to this marvellous woman and hope she feels appreciated for a day or two at least.

So you did hear about Giovanna and the school billet? Well I guess in all fairness I should refresh your vague memory, as I've been so bossy about you being open on this subject. By the by, I did just happen to notice the evasions in your last letter about the troubles Dave mentioned. But no more about that. Well, on with this story. We went away on one of those inter-school sports exchanges which old McIntyre, the sports master, reckoned were so good for us. I was on the swim team, Giovanna on the hockey team. There was some mix up, with one billeting family having to pull out at the last minute. But the family which had agreed to take me said they could accommodate another girl. The relieved teachers didn't ask too many questions, so Giovanna and I turned up at this farm together. Didn't know each other all that well, she was a few years junior to me, but because I was in the same class as Dave we got on OK. Which is just as well, 'cause the family we went to had three boys. They were disgusted at having to play host to two girls and barely spoke to us the whole time. The father rarely came in off the tractor before eight o'clock in the evenings and had left the house by six each morning. The mother tried really hard to transform the household into something like warm hospitality, but it was beyond any woman. She obviously felt embarrassed by the poverty of the farm, and the boys' terse hostility, but it was all too hard to fix at the end of her extremely long days working as farmer, farm accountant, mother and general skivvy. She did produce huge and comforting meals, and after a strenuous day's sport Giovanna and I were very grateful for her generous cooking. I've never eaten so much baked pumpkin.

Anyway, after these huge meals, we'd help to wash up, and then there was nothing to do. They didn't have a television, and conversation wasn't an option for any of us. So we'd retreat to the bedroom – where we had to share a double bed. Not sure if the school knew about this arrangement but there it was. I remember being taken aback to discover that there were no sheets. Although our family wasn't well off, the realisation that whole families slept without any sheets, ever, impressed my naive teenage mind enormously. So, using the excuse of our need for an early night, Giovanna and I would climb into our Spartan bed. As it was a region of frosts and the house had no heating, we cuddled up from necessity. On the first night, as we were getting changed, ready for bed, I glimpsed Giovanna's extraordinary and beautiful breasts. She was a very womanly fifteen-year-old. Coming from a long line of small-breasted women, I was fascinated. As she snuggled in bed with me, wriggling urgently to get as close as possible to my body heat, I felt them jostling against my back. For the first time in my life I felt a potent desire to run my fingers along every centimetre of her water-brown, muscular flesh. I just wanted and wanted to touch her. Most especially to feel those breasts, their weight in my hands, to see if I could produce changes to the shape of those mushroom-velvet nipples. I'd felt occasional flickers of desire for other girls but not this rushing lust. So, being direct and forthright (and just a little thoughtless!) even then, I asked her if she'd mind, and to my amazement she said no, she didn't mind. After that, we spent glorious hours stroking and kissing each other's breasts, and tongue kissing with great enthusiasm. We agreed not to touch anything below the waists of our pyjamas as that would definitely earn the disapproval of Father Doherty, who was Giovanna's blood and thunder priest.

We were woken each morning by a startling pre-dawn drop in temperature, and the sounds of the farmer getting ready for his day's work. This gave us the chance to indulge for another hour or so, luxuriating in the paradoxical softness and firmness of fit women's bodies ... an opportunity we energetically embraced ... surfing each other like sleek dolphins. Needless to say neither of us performed on the sports field or in the swimming pool as well as expected. We were too exhausted by our late night and early morning performances ... though we knew no-one was going to award us any medals or trophies for that kind of performance, except maybe the burning badge of scandalised disapproval. On the bus trip home Giovanna got hit by a huge attack of guilt and sobbed against my willing shoulder. I didn't know quite what to make of it all. The experience had felt so right, like swimming in cold surf on a humid day ... but I knew it wasn't regarded as normal. Also, I was worried about Giovanna. If her father or oily Father Doherty ever found out, she'd be in serious trouble. So on this miserable, rowdy bus trip, we whisperingly agreed that we wouldn't do it again, ever. I also convinced Giovanna that as we hadn't touched each other below the waistline, we'd committed no sin, so she didn't need to make a confession about it. Not sure about the theology of this, but even at seventeen I knew that the consequences of confessing to this gentle, innocent pleasuring would be obscene and probably dangerous for Giovanna.

After that, we'd smile obliquely at one another in the school grounds. I made a point of always watching her hockey team play. Loved to see her rich brown eyes and intelligent face bud-tight with concentration as she chased and dodged over the field. Her robust movements as she ran pleasurably reminded me of our sheetless nights. But I didn't ever approach her again, and the year after that I left school. So that was my first time ... what about yours? Will you tell me sometime? Maybe on your back verandah one velvet night?

You did get the flight details I left on your answering machine last week, didn't you? I'm so looking forward to it that I've started packing already, instead of leaving it till the last minute. Miracles will never cease. I will have to go shopping for some swimmers when I get up there though. When I got mine out to pack, I realised that they'd suddenly gone all saggy. I'm sure they looked fine when I went away to the reunion, but in the intervening weeks the bad-swimmer fairy has been in and zapped all the elastic and the smooth black has perished into gritty grey worms. Do you remember how we used to go on regular shopping expeditions for swimmers when we were younger? I laugh to remember the way we used to go together for moral support. We'd stand beside each other in all those seedy change rooms where the mirrors stood in stern judgement, condemning the most innocent of dimples as heinous cellulite and funny waist-expanding angles as the truth of middle-aged spread. And we'd stand there repeating the mantras: 'You have a fine, healthy, normal woman's body', 'There's nothing wrong with being a size sixteen', 'That's just a very unflattering cut', 'The mirrors in here distort' and so on. Then when we'd finally bought a pair each, we'd race to the nearest coffee shop and have milky coffee and the fattest, richest cake available, laughing and snorting as we recalled our encounters with all those thin, judgmental, teenage shop assistants and those gross judgmental mirrors lit like concentration camps. What satisfaction we felt when we won the day and found swimmers that were affordable, suitable for comfortable swimming, and looked OK. Do you remember that ritual? 'When shopping for swimmers or underclothes it is advisable to do so in supportive pairs.' That sign should be plastered above the doors of all shop changing rooms, don't you think? Otherwise you can get so flustered, rushing home with some ill-fitting purchase, all hot-faced and bothered just because of the thoughtless remarks of a size eight shop assistant.

Lord, I didn't mean to rattle on so long, meant this to just quickly let you know I'd received your last letter and to confirm that you'd received the flight details. Can't quite believe we'll be there in a few short days. Am so excited at the thought of hearing your stories, your voice, and best of all, hugging you ... see you SOON —

Love from Molly.

Dearest Molly,

Was horrible to get your desperate phone call so early this morning, to hear the pain and shock in your voice. There's no easy way to hear of a mother's death but the late night phone call must be one of the worst. I guess there is a tiny granule of consolation in knowing that it was fast, if they said she'd died before they got her to the hospital. But poor you ... and what about Leigh? Only that one exam to sit, and she'd have been finished. I think it was wise not to let her sit it though, straight after a shock like that. How's your Dad? Do hope he's not trying to be all Stoic and strong, it'd be so much better if he just let others do the coping and wailed for a few days, but it would probably go against the grain for someone like him, used to being reliable in all weathers.

S'pose it was some kind of luck that you were able to use the airline tickets you'd already booked to get to Brisbane quickly. A pity Ania couldn't go with you. Or did you prefer that, wanting to go through it alone with just Leigh and your Dad as companions? Can't help kicking the door frames with frustration though when I think of the blissful holiday you'd planned, a respite after the tough swim you've been doing lately, and now this. Don't the fates know when to let up?

And I rage at the waste of Ruby, she was still so fresh and open about every aspect of life. Can't help bitterly asking "Why?". But of course there is no reasoning with death, it just wanders into the kitchen, familiar as the kid next door, licks the icing bowl clean and leaves. And one of the things that's weirdest is that although it changes everything, everything also looks the same on the surface. I remember thinking, the day after my mother died, how can it be a normal sunny day, with everyone going off to work, the bread truck doing its rounds, my body needing ordinary attentions, and the whole rigmarole going on as if nothing had happened. But it did, and I did, and twenty something years down that particular unchosen path, some of the strangeness has worn off.

As you know I'm not flat out at work at present, so if you'd like me to come down to Brisbane and help, you know I'd dive down there without pause. Friends like me can be useful for taking your Dad to appointments when you need a break, or taking boxes of clothes to the Salvos when you can't face it, or taking Leigh for long walks so that you don't have to be lifeguard support person to the world, as well as doing your own grieving. So, if any of those things sound like they might help right now, just say and I'll book myself straight down to you.

Don't know what else to say. Can only beg that if you want to ring, at ANY time, to talk or just to hear my voice and be reminded that there are still women in the world who love you, please don't hesitate. I send you enveloping hugs, and will be in touch soon — love to you and Leigh, always,

Finn

P.S. Give Bill a loving hug from me too, tell him I'm thinking of him.

Dear Molly,

Thanks for ringing, I had been so worried about you, and Leigh, bobbing about in your badly listing coracle of grief. Sounds like you're paddling extremely well though, in the rough circumstances. Identifying the body must have been the worst. And I guess you'll have to be in Brisbane for the coroner's inquest? Maybe it would be good if I came down to be your scaffolding then? Think about it. Of course, it will depend on work and other factors as to whether I'm able to get away, but I'd like to be there if I could. Sounds wonderful the way Leigh and your Dad are relating, healing for both of them, but best of all, it takes some of the pressure off you. The ceremony by the river with the red wine and the dark red roses sounds like an inspired way to farewell a feisty red-blooded woman like Ruby. I feel the urgency of tears as I write that, how I wish I could do something to ease the pain ... do you really want a copy of that piece I wrote? Words seem so feeble in the face of this stuff. Since you asked for it, I'll enclose it, but I won't expect you to read it, so don't feel obliged.

Rang and had a long talk with Ania last night, my oblique way of helping you. She sounded fine, though shocked and worried. When are you planning to get back to the mountains? Or is it too soon to decide that yet? And what arrangements have to be made about Leigh's exam?

Questions, questions, when probably what you want are soothing answers. Ring again when you can.

Love you — Finn

Melbourne Weather Forecasts

cloudy 1

resurrected an old poem of mine it was trying to bid farewell
to grief
as if you could
made me laugh right up loud to see my naive hope
that one poem could reef this old companion
from my bed my life my every move

muggy

read one of those calendar quotes
it said everyday life's about loss one way or another
because change and loss go hand in hand
or some other bloody cliche
but i guess it's true
don't you hate it when you agree with the desk calendar

cloud bursts 2

went out to dinner with a friend she'd just been hit
by a double-decker bus-size grief first time in her life
she wanted to know if i knew about such things
when I told her my sad-story she seemed truly shocked
as if i'd told her i could still walk
when in fact i'd lost both legs

sudden wind gusts

i've seen this look of shock before
my sisters and i often laugh about it in an odd grim way
how people innocently ask about parents and we tell
and they don't know what to say and neither do we
even hardened psychiatrists start fiddling
with their tissue boxes
as if some basket-cases were really beyond
their basket-weaving talents
and they wish we'd gone to see someone else

still cloudy 3

didn't dare tell her about
getting the Double-Orphan's pension when I was at uni
i think it's kind of funny but not many others do
i mean the name is so Dickensian ridiculous
that sentimental phrase Double-Orphan
written on those absolutely DSS forms

some showers
my friend seemed awed by my story she's hurting now
i'd like to help but how
another friend of mine reckons i've got a PhD in grief
i'm so bloody expert at it
huh is what i say to that

rainclouds 4
what to say it changes and just as you lose landmarks in your life
that you thought would always be there
so you lose the pain that you think will always be there
and just as bloody well
cause you can't go on feeling so amputated
and no-one seems to notice
or they just want to step around
the pool of blood you leave wherever you go
or hand you a tinsy little tissue to clean up the mess
when can't they see
you're bloody haemorrhaging

sunburst through cloud 5
i was pretty impressed with what she did with her grief though
came to our workshop and passed her pain and anger and
bitter questions and other chaotic feelings around
on life-full leaves of exquisite tissue-paper
she is brave and wise

cloud-cover 6
made me want to weep and cheer and hug her
and pile them up and admire them slowly piece
by piece wasn't quite the right space so i said
sensible supportive things
but i was proud of her and a little bit envious
it was so much smarter
than running to the other side of the world alone
pretending you were normal and
stuffing all those words and feelings down inside you
packing them in till you felt like one big gum boil
that's what i did
it took 13 years a huge effort and a skilled grief-surgeon
to clean up and
get me anywhere near fully functioning again

scattered cloud 7

want to see the scars
laugh and lift my shirt
have you read that book women who run with wolves
she writes about belonging to the Scar Clan
really made me and my sisters laugh
we reckon we're 3rd generation Scar Clan
and every now and then we feel sort of proud of the fact
that we are still alive and functioning
at least most of us most of the time and
some people aren't even aware of how much
all that scar tissue binds us together

cloud lifting 8

and that's what i want to say to my new-wound friend
that you hate it and fight it and wish it away
like you do a persistent cat that wakes you
when you are suicide-desperate for sleep
but it is here to stay
and sometime when you're not even looking
you remember how to laugh
and the scars are there
but they do stop suppurating eventually
and come clean shiny healthy-looking
well as healthy as a big scar can look and
that will happen faster for her because of the brave wise way
she's attending to those wounds
while they are still fresh-hurting
and she will just go on feeling less awful
and better able to laugh
even though she can't imagine it right now

and finally tomorrow's forecast

it's kind of like Melbourne weather
unpredictable
but it just keeps going on and on
and a lot of us go on living there
in spite of it
being like that

November 16

Dear Finn,

Thanks for the two letters you sent to Brisbane. Saved me, really. Made me think of parachute silk. That billowing strength. The sensual lifesaving shapes keeping me aloft when utter plummeting seemed so much more likely. Your words – tough as parachute silk and as thoroughly comforting.

I thought I'd been through some rough stuff before but nothing prepares you for this death. Everything feels smashed and quivering and wherever I turn, a sliver of memory gashes me in the most unsuspecting places. Got back to the mountains last night and all I can manage today is to slump in a chair under the pear tree and gaze at its leaves and the two king parrots paddling in them. And now, after a few hours of that, I've mustered the strength to assemble pen and paper and start to write to you. Feel so feeble and listless. Like what is the point of anything any more? Ania rang all my clients and moved their appointments to next week, so I've got about five days (big deal!) respite before I have to start making sense and looking whole. Seems an impossible ask from where I'm slumped but everyone raves about the miraculous effects of time, so I'm hoping they're right – but five days!?

Felt very torn about coming back. Part of me wanted to stay with Dad and help him finish all the urgent tidying, cook him meals and just generally be there for him. But another part of me longed to be back here in my own bed, with my own Ania, away from the constant pain. The Brisbane house is (was?) so much Ruby's house, I couldn't do even the simplest thing, like go to the toilet, without being reminded of her, and the abyss left by her absence. Also worried that too much of that was not a good thing for Leigh, though in the end she decided to stay up there another week to help Dad sort through Ruby's things. God, I hope she'll be OK. She was very clear that she'd be fine, and would leave if it started to get too heavy. One thing I must tell you, I've asked them not to hurl too many things 'cause I remember your tales of doing a big cleansing toss-out after your mother's death, only to regret it later. Any comfort in knowing that others learn from your mistakes?

Glad we did the red ceremony by ourselves, because the funeral proper was a shemozzle. Lots of people wanted to say something, which was fine, but some of it was mawkish and pseudo-godly in a way that I think Ruby would have hated. Imagined her sitting in the back pew having a sardonic laugh at us all. But ... I guess if it helped them then it was good, but as a ritual I found it infuriating rather than useful. No place for me, no real space for celebrating the mother I knew. Perhaps I'm just not ready for any of it yet. You're certainly spot-on about the irrational questions. I keep waking up in a fury, arguing with faceless judges about why they shouldn't take MY mother. Bill gets a lot of consolation from the fact that it was so quick, keeps telling me, 'That's how your mother wanted to go, fast, no fuss, no maundering on, no maudlin death-bed scenes'. He's right, but whenever he says that, it takes all my strength not to shout at him, 'OK, that's great, it was a neat kind of death, but why did it have to be NOW? She could have had the kind of death she wanted, but twenty years later!' Of course I can't say that to him and diminish the one source of comfort he's got but ... and I feel so guilty when I get angry with him ... I know it's not his fault, any of it ... and I can't even get too furious with the driver whose brakes failed ... poor young bloke ... bet he's feeling like hell right now too. He sent a little note via the police, to say how sorry he was ... a pale little notelet with a few daffodils and faltering words on it. Could almost feel the sweat of his distress coming off that flimsy paper. Had to admire him for trying. What could he say? It's so huge.

It turns out that Ruby decided to take out life insurance for herself and Bill about five years ago. So apparently there'll be some kind of pay out. Find it hard to focus on that sort of idiocy. All those lists of body parts rated at so many dollars per square centimetre. Bizarre. How could you ever dollar-value the loss of a woman like Ruby, splendid mother, partner, grandmother ... not to mention all she gave to the community? Now I begin to sound like her obituary and I'm out of energy. Can see I'll have to go back to staring at the leaves ... thanks for being there and listening so lovingly.

Will be in touch soon – Molly.

Dear Molly,

Pleased to know that you're back home, harbouring under the pear tree. Have you heard from Leigh yet? It does seem a lot for someone so tender to manage, but then again, she's had you for a mother and, I've noticed, our daughters are tougher than we are sometimes. And maybe some quiet companionable time with Bill will allow them to give solace to each other. As you know, there's no right way to travel through such events. Think of all the people who are convinced that they're right, and then think about the hideous messes they make. So, although it sounds impossible, can you try to stop worrying about everyone else and just do things that help you? Please?

Decided to have an early night last night, after a long day of marking essays and calculating results. So I ran a bath brimful with relaxing oils, wallowed in it for a while, embracing thoughts of you, then went to slide into my celebrated waterbed. Only guess what? It had sprung a leak! So instead of a relaxing early night, Angus and I had to spend the next few hours emptying the slimy plastic bladder, finding the repair kit, finding and mending the hole, drying everything we could reach, filling the bladder up again, arguing about how full it should be (always a source of disagreement), finding some fresh dry sheets, making the bed all over again, and then, about midnight we were able to climb gingerly into it. And all this, after I sent you that celebratory rave about the joy of waterbeds.

Funerals are bizarre experiences. I've never been to one that did the cathartic release of grief bit. Last one I went to, I left after fifteen minutes. Lola, who was about 5, was howling, so that was my excellent excuse, but I was really glad to go. There was something very distressing to me that day about being in one room with so many people exuding powerful emotions. Wonder how many people, given the choice, would sneak out the side door halfway through? But maybe it's better to stay put and go through the whole gamut. I don't know. But more urgently I want to know, what are you currently doing — for you? You're right — five days is a tiny amount of time to get some kind of perspective on a mother's death, but it's better than nothing. At least you're not a single mother with four kids having to go back to work the day after the funeral in order to feed everyone. Don't mean to sound horribly unsympathetic, but do make the most of your free time while it's there. You need to use every second of it wisely if you're going to keep shouldering the kinds of responsibilities you have in your life. Can't see you being content with staring at leaves forever. And it doesn't pay well.

Speaking of shoulders and money, I've enclosed some indulgence dollars in this letter ... I'd strongly suggest spending it on a full-body massage ... they are wonderful things for comforting mother-hungry bodies and sagging lifeguards. But there may be something else you'd rather indulge in, a deep red shirt to wear on your first day back at work to give you courage, and to remind you of Ruby's blood-deep strength, or ... did you ever go to see that counsellor you spoke about? Whatever — you decide — the only prescriptions that come with it are: (i) don't spend it on onions and toilet-paper; and (ii) when you spend it, remember that I love you and am wrapping both arms round you, full-strength.

Have you even begun to think what you might do at Christmas? It's going to be a terrible and a tough one, so start preparing early. Talk to me soon. Am enclosing a rather simple poem I wrote recently, just because I thought it might provide a gentle place to float your weary mind. Wish I could offer more.

Love and hugs — Finn

a glass of water and a bed with clean sheets

if i were to confect a new religion? what rules?
i'm not keen on rules
i think maybe no rules well perhaps one strict one
No Deliberate Hurting
how's that for a holy original start?
after that a list of suggestions like
lie under a big old tree once a day and gaze the bellying branches
map their sky sculpture and suss the undersea swells of light and air and
how about everyone stops work at 2 o'clock in the afternoon to
enjoy blameless and relaxing sex or a full-body massage and
dive reverent into fragrant sea lake creek or large bath whenever possible and
spade chop through the flesh of a mouldy rockmelon once a week
imagining the melon is the pleading head of a worst enemy and
holding hands with an intimate for 10 minutes
might become a compulsory daily ritual as might
playing ludicrous games with children and learning their logic
and the bible? well there wouldn't be one
everyone would be given a practical and beautiful notebook as well as
millionaire's time in which to write and draw their own
philosophies music stories sightings dreams fables riddles recipes epiphanies fears
their personal climatic conditions
all the cyclonic impulses low depressions gale-force highs and
anything else they discovered in the playground of their minds and
i'd redefine the sacred to include all the everyday tea-leaf-sized revelations
that you don't need 3 years alone on a rock snow hillside eating dhal to appreciate
like aren't you glad to wake up on a breath-easy morning without a sore back?
isn't that something to reverence?
like friends who can cook
work you like
bearable parents
easy masturbation
absent fear
understandable children
access to books
they're all worth a bit of celebration aren't they?
could go on but i'll stop and let you add your particular sacreds
do you reckon it'd find followers?
may need some modifications some irony but i'm post-massage
why'd you ask me such a serious question at a time when bliss seems simple and
a glass of water and a bed with clean sheets
most worthy of worship?

November 30

Dear Finn

Found your letter a bit, um, bracing at first, but then anything and everything hurts right now. After sitting under the pear tree and reading it a couple of times, I can see that perhaps you're right to be a bit stern with me.

Anyway, after reading your letter a number of times I rang Ania and arranged to take her out to dinner, by way of celebrating the good things that I have left in my life. Before we did that, she managed to get away from school early, and we went shopping, with Ruby in mind and your money in hand. Didn't see any special shirts but did find a pair of dark-red linen trousers which I bought (actually had my size ... and they're a comfortable fit!) and will wear them on the first day back at work, as you suggested. If my heart does a serious wobble, at least my legs will be clad in the strength of two good women. Also bought a slender red-glass vase from a funny second-hand shop, which I'll sit on my desk as another reminder of Ruby.

Leigh got back this morning, and I feel so relieved, hearing her round the house, and knowing that at least at this instant she is safe. Had nightmares about her being killed while she was in Brisbane, stupid, I know, but if it can happen to a mother, it can happen to a precious daughter, can't it? Logic is such a shaky concept, don't you think? And talking the law of averages is no help at all to the grief-stricken.

The poem was peaceful, and I enjoyed most of it, except the line about 'bearable parents' ... which I thought was a bit tactless in the circumstances. But I took it in the spirit in which you sent it. You're pretty good at the art of gentle admonishment, did you know that?

Can't quite get my head around Christmas, though I know you're right. Will talk to Dad about it tomorrow when he rings. He's sounding amazingly solid. Sad, really sad, but doing resourceful things, like writing letters and notes to Ruby every day in a special notebook he bought. Would you mind if I sent him a copy of that poem? Think he'd get a blast out of it, especially the stuff about multiple biblical notebooks instead of The One & Only Bible.

Leigh seems incredibly serene after her time in Brisbane. Sometimes can't quite line up this vision of an elegant, calm, young woman with the intense memory of that clinging baby at my breast. Guess all parents have this problem at times ... and now she's actually taller than me and has taken to calling me 'Shortie'. Only from a daughter! The best news is that she doesn't have to sit another exam. Apparently they average out her year's work in that subject, or do some other complicated mathematics, and arrive at a grade that way. Isn't that humane? Not quite what I expect from large government departments, but I'm not complaining. It's just such a relief that it's all sorted and we don't have to do anything more.

Have taken up my swimming again ... feels really creaky and my joints complained raucously the first few mornings, but I feel Ruby's strong brown hand pushing me into the pool, and you standing by, rewarding me with a warm towel embrace at the end. Day before yesterday, I literally bumped into a woman who was also doing laps, and she cracked me hard on the nose with the down-stroke of her over-arm. She apologised and then swam on. So did I, but by the time I'd reached the other end of the pool, the pain in my face was jiving with all the other pain I'm feeling and I couldn't swallow back the howls and sobs any longer. Grabbed the lane rope, of course it had to be at the deep end, and clung there, blubbering like an abandoned child. Was so racked (now I really know the meaning of the word) I couldn't even co-ordinate my arms to pull myself out of the pool. The woman, who'd clocked me, stopped and asked if I was all right. Well clearly I wasn't! But I said it wasn't just the effect of the blow on the nose, and I'd be fine. She didn't seem convinced, but swam off, finished her laps and then went and spoke to the lifeguard.

He came over, took one look at my snotty face and said, 'Don't think you'll be doing any more laps today, will you? I mumbled 'No', and he said, 'Here, grab on', reached down his sculpted muscular arms, and flipped me out of the pool as efficiently as a fisherman landing a cod. Then there was the problem of moving from the poolside to the change-rooms. The lifeguard went and got my gear, wrapped my towel round my shoulders and offered to bring me a cup of tea. You know how it is, when someone's unexpectedly kind — my sobs intensified. He read that as a yes and ambled off. He came back with a really sugary, milky concoction which I managed to gulp down, mainly out of politeness. You know I hate tea at the best of times. But it did seem to have a good effect because a few minutes later I was able to gather all my stuff together and shuffle a shaky retreat to the women's change rooms where I had the longest hot shower. I felt such an idiot. Thankfully it was still pretty early so the pool wasn't packed. On my way out, I found the courage to go and thank the lifeguard, and he said, 'That's all right, I've got three sisters', as if that explained everything, which in a way maybe it did. Drove home slowly, and crawled into bed for the rest of the morning. Grief is a bizarre experience, isn't it? When do you stop feeling so fragile and unpredictable?

Best away, Leigh and I are going shopping for something for her to commemorate Ruby this afternoon and I want to post this then. Hope all is steady at your end,

Lots of love from Molly.

7th December

Dear Molly,

The bad news about fragility is that it quivers you around for a damn long time. In my case there were about fifteen years following mum's death where a piece of jazz that she'd loved dancing to, or the sight of an iris flowering in someone's garden, could transform me from solid, adult, woman-of-the-world to whimpering toddler in seconds. So you mustn't expect it to disappear quickly. Glad you got such a sympathetic lifeguard — talk about lucky! Have you been back to the pool since then? I hope so. You mustn't let a trivial emotion like embarrassment stop you doing something as restorative as swimming. You haven't, have you?

How's it been, going back to work? Did you have to tell all your clients what had happened? That would be tough. Or did Ania tell them when she rang to shift their appointments? Hope so. I can remember having to write letters to all the far away friends listed in mum's address book, letting them know she'd died, and just the fact of having to write that unpalatable fact over and over again was like rubbing sand into a weeping chafe. That and having to clean out her bathroom cupboard ... they were the worst ... she had a nearly new toothbrush. God, how I howled when I found that. Sounds silly, doesn't it? But I guess it's like trying to explain the logic of your outpouring at the pool the other day. Grief grabs ordinary things, words, events, and converts them into another, completely idiosyncratic code. Most times it's explicable to no-one, least of all you. After a while, after fighting and trying to explain it, I just gave up. I accepted that the logic of grief, like the logic of what makes kids tick, was beyond explanation. I found the only thing to do was to surrender to its inexorable codes and once I did that, I had more strength for shuffling back into normal life on the occasions when grief let me. A bit like when you get caught in a savage rip at the surf. Instead of trying to swim against it you have to flow with it a way and then swim sidewards to extricate yourself from its grip when it loses some of its ferocity. It can mean a long swim back, often to a different beach from the one you left. That in itself is disorienting — but not as disorienting as drowning.

After much flailing about, we've decided to stay put for Christmas. Angus feels a bit guilty about obligations to his family, but the thought of staying home and cooking up a tropical feast in his own kitchen and having a really pressure-free break was too tempting. Also money's a bit tricky just now and there's some disquieting stuff happening at work, so we'll stay home and conserve all our resources, emotional as well as financial. How are your plans shaping up for the festive season, given that it won't be for you this time around? Would you all like to come up for a holiday on The Island, something completely different to the Brisbane tradition? You know, don't you, that we'd love to see you, including Bill ... why don't you suggest it to him? I could do accommodation bookings and so forth to take some of the hassle out of it for you. Let me know.

Better slope off now, I'm due to go to an examiners' meeting where we finalise results — they're always pretty gruelling. So I'll empty my bladder, change my tampon and latch my face on straight — or the consequences could be dire.

Wish I were sitting under the pear tree giving you a hand massage and helping you learn how to laugh again.

Take good care of you —

Love from Finn

December 16

Dear Finn

Liked your idea about the hand massage so much, that the
Saturday after getting your letter I coaxed Leigh down
under the pear tree with a bottle of Ruby's favourite
almond and honey hand-cream. We sat there for a couple
of hours, taking it in turns to massage each other's hands,
chatting in no particular direction, even laughing
occasionally, watching the liquid light in the new summer
foliage. It was one of those glittery mountain days when
everything looks as if it's outlined in silver eye shadow.
There, see you how you lure me to lyricism with your
suggestions? No, but it was a lovely afternoon and I felt
really restored by Leigh's gentle strength as she worked at
unfurling my hands. Just loved being with her. Sat scanning
the distinctive nuances of her hairline, the way the hairs
whorl with the precision of expensive chocolates. Listening
to her laughter, so like Ruby's. She seems uncannily calm
about everything. Of course I both admire, and worry
about, that. Mothers!

Going back to work has been pretty tough, as you so
accurately forecast. I still feel a great sense of surprise
when I look in the mirror and see myself there, looking like
a competent, active woman. It simply doesn't match up at
all with the pale jelly woman whose miseries keep
splattering strange patterns all over the walls. Fortunately,
the rest of the world seems convinced by the mirror
woman, so with a great effort of faith and will I sustain her.
Some days that's easier than others, and I'm grateful that
she exists, at least in mirrors and other people's minds.
Other days the jelly woman wants to take over. She can be
quite fierce and determined. I have to devise clever
strategies for giving her some private space, so that she

doesn't splot out in the middle of a session with one of my clients. Saturday mornings have become her time. I don't do my swim and just lie in bed, looking at photo albums or reading Ruby's letters. Or I write in my journal in the voice of the jelly woman, asking all the irrational questions, like 'why me', letting out all the 'I want my mother' howls and guilt-soaked memories of times when I failed her in some way.

Leigh and Ania quite cheerfully vacate the house when the jelly woman waddles out. Understandably, they find Saturday morning shopping far easier to cope with than her. And that's fine with me. I find it's difficult to be considerate when you're in the grip of savage grief. By the time the other two return, I've usually showered, returned my face to something resembling the usual me, and the jelly woman is content to be quiet for a while. Then I'm able to face washing the clothes, unpacking the shopping, helping Leigh with her stuff and talking over Ania's school politics – all in all looking quite normal – but it can only happen after I've made peace with the jelly woman and given her some of the attention she craves.

Does that sound absolutely mad to you? Possibly it is, but then grief is a pretty unbalancing experience, so I figure maybe doing something equally unbalanced is best. Do you think? Like homoeopathy where they actually administer minuscule doses of the poison which is making you ill and it works like a kind of inoculation? So maybe acting delirious in contained bursts will prevent me from spinning off into a zillion fragments? I do, fairly desperately, fear losing touch with that mirror woman that everyone else seems to believe in. What do you think?

Onto slightly less grim matters – Christmas plans. After your suggestion of a tropical retreat at Christmas, I spoke to Dad about it. He liked the idea of not being in Brisbane, which was a relief to me. I just didn't think I could face it. When I mentioned your idea of us all going to The Island he got really excited about spending Christmas on another island, the one where he and mum spent their honeymoon. Could be painful I guess, but also an apt way to celebrate the ending of their relationship, to go back to the place where it sort of started. Anyway he sounded really energised about it, and as I figure I'm going to be miserable wherever we spend it, I said, 'Yes, let's look into it'. So he's going to see the local travel agent and then let me know whether it's feasible or not. Course it may not be affordable for all four of us to go. I'm not sure how flush Dad is after the funeral and so forth, and I've missed a few weeks work in recent months so I'm a bit skint, but we'll see. We won't be doing what you suggested, but one of your good ideas has sparked off another. You're a bollard, you know that?

Love to you, Lola and Angus, but especial hugs to you. The jelly woman and I miss you very badly right now.

Molly.

Dear Molly,

Saw this card and thought of you and your swimming, so here it is. Not really a Christmas card, just a "thinking of you" kind of card. Great to hear your voice last night and find out your plans. As you know I've been worried. Going to Lord Howe Island sounds very seemly, as you put it. It is such a beautiful place, and although that won't take away the miseries, there is something just a little consoling about huge tree-swaddled mountains and vast stretches of ocean. Especially as you know it as a place in which your mum was truly happy. I think she'd be impressed that you were going there to commemorate her. And I know money worries you, but there's that insurance payout pending, isn't there? I can just imagine Ruby chortling approvingly at you spending her life insurance on an island Christmas extravaganza. Leigh will love it, I'm sure, and she's had a choppy eventful year all round too. Can imagine Bill and Leigh heading off on invigorating, virtue-inducing bushwalks, while you and Ania slide down to the beach to do impersonations of somnolent sea slugs. Sounds enjoyable ... possibly?

As my tribute to Ruby, I thought I'd try to make, for Christmas dinner, that wonderful cake she used to produce on special occasions. You know the one, with grated chocolate, hazelnuts and black cherries in it? Is there any chance of you sending me a copy of her recipe before you depart, please? If it's not easy, don't fuss about it. I just thought it would be a happy way to enjoy her memory.

Am out of space, ring me soon, before you leave, or from the island, reverse the charges if the phones are complicated.

Missing you heaps — love — Finn

Lord Howe Island

December 26

Dear Finn

Well, we survived Christmas day. You're right about this island's effect. It's not easy to remain glum when surrounded by such grandeur. And you know I'm not one for singing about the joys of nature. Not like some other hippy-type person we both know and love. Yesterday was fairly tough, but we did it. Swam in the morning, at a beach where Dad and Ruby had done salacious things with each other in the sand-hills! Such admissions he's been making on this trip! A revelation to all of us. I think Leigh's quite startled to hear such tales from Grandpa, but it won't do her any harm to realise that an interest in sex isn't the sole preserve of the very young. Then we went to one of the resorts for lunch. I found it a strain, being shut up with a whole lot of other people and their bonhomie. But soon after we arrived and Ania saw the tension on my face, she explained our situation to a waiter and asked if we could have a table outside. He whisked around with great efficiency, and we were seated out on a terrace in minutes. I feel so grateful to have people like Ania around when I'm still so inert in the face of even small challenges.

After that, we had as enjoyable a lunch as possible, given Ruby's absence. We set a place for her and poured her a glass of champagne as we drank to her memory. I had an extra glass for the jelly woman, who is a demon for champagne, and she was reasonably well behaved until we got back to the apartment. Then she demanded a sob session on the bed. Ania lay beside me and stroked my back until the jelly subsided, and we both slept for a while. When I woke up, I could hear Dad snoring and Leigh attempting to prowl quietly. So I crept out and together we snuck off for another swim. Both felt much clearer after dousing ourselves in icy water and having our torpor pummelled out of us by the rough surf. Walked the length of the beach together, a pass-time we've loved since she was tiny, talking along, or being silent, and showing each other things we find in the sea wrack. Last night, I even managed to sleep quite well, which hasn't been happening as often as it might.

Sorry I didn't get the recipe to you before we left, it was all too much. But Bill brought a copy with him, so I'll enclose it with this. Maybe you can bake it for New Year celebrations, she suggests hopefully. How was your Christmas anyway? We're staying on here till the 3rd, so I'll call you after that.

Love you – Molly.

Ruby's Special Occasion Cake

180 gms or $^2/_3$ cup sugar
200 gms butter
3 eggs
100 gms dark cooking chocolate (grated)
125 gms hazelnuts (ground)
125 gms or 1 slightly heaped cup self-raising flour
3 tablespoons brown rum
1 bottle or large tin pitted black cherries
   (very well drained)
Some extra rum

Heat the oven to 170°C. Butter an 8-cup capacity cake tin. Grind hazelnuts to medium fine in a food processor. The chocolate can either be grated by hand on a coarse cheese grater or added to the hazelnuts in the processor, but won't need as long in the processor as the hazelnuts. The chocolate should have been refrigerated before either grating or processing, otherwise it melts and sticks.

Cream the butter and sugar together until pale golden. Add eggs one at a time to creamed mixture. Mix in sifted flour, rum, grated chocolate and ground hazelnuts. Pour into prepared cake tin. It will be quite a stiff mixture. Take the drained cherries and gently press into the top of the cake, leaving half a cheek showing. Bake for about 1+ hour. Remove from oven when cooked (test with a clean metal skewer) and place on a cake rack to cool. Whilst cake is still very hot trickle the extra rum over it. Best, if possible, to leave the cake overnight and serve the following day, as this allows the flavours to develop. It is not a complicated or messy cake to make but always tastes delicious, especially when served with whipped cream.

Dear Molly,

As you say, given the prevailing emotional weather conditions, that sounds as good a Christmas Day as you could possibly hope for. How I envied you that (em)bracing swim at the end of the day. It was 33°C here and very muggy, and you know how tepid the ocean is, like swimming in luke-warm washing-up water. How I long for a proper surf. Earlier in the week we checked the weather forecast and decided to head for the rainforest for Christmas Day. Cooked up a variety of different favourites on Christmas Eve, including one of Angus' famous chicken pies, a mango and avocado salad and a lemon tart. Lola was up early on the day, surprise, surprise! We opened the presents, had a quick breakfast, then packed the car and headed to the nearest mountain range. It was at least 10° cooler than at home, and we found our favourite swimming hole completely unpeopled. So spent an idyllic day, swimming, exploring the rocks (you know how Lola loves to climb), eating intermittently, watching the fish feed, and finally just lying still, admiring the way the water went sliding over the rocks. Lola had been given a new mask and snorkel so she spent ages lusciously mermaiding about with her head underwater, investigating the habits of freshwater yabbies. It was so peaceful. We didn't get home till after six that night.

Friends had pressed us to call by sometime during the day, for a Christmas drink, so we stopped in on our way home. They were in the midst of quarrelling over whether it was too early to prepare the evening meal, and the tension in the air was enough to fuel a hot-air balloon. They were surprised and not-so-secretly horrified to see us. Everyone looked hot and homicidal, their skins stretched balloon-tight from eating and drinking too much. The kids were longing for bed but had imbibed so much sugar they were mainlining on mayhem. The inter-generational differences were being magnified by the mugginess, and conflict over parenting styles looked set to spark World War III. We felt as comfortable as greenies at a Forestry Industry convention. We accepted a beer each, tried to prevent Lola drinking the litre of Coke she was offered, and slid out of there as rapidly as we could.

Went home with a strong sense of relief that for once we'd resisted the sentimental push for a big Family Christmas, and done something really enjoyable and simple. Maybe Christmas Day should be renamed Duty Day. So many people I know endure the most complicated and horrific Xmas days because of a sense of duty ... and the weirdest thing is that the poor old parents do it because they think their adult children still want it, while the kids do it because they think their parents want it ... do you see this happening? Or is it just my bitter double-orphan's eye that makes it appear this way? However cynical my view may be, can't help feeling that for most people the celebratory concept of Christmas has been completely mouldered away by deathly rituals and the heavy cobwebbing of commercialism. If it really is about the year turning over, about new life and hope beginning, better to go bush and enjoy what's freely on offer. And that's my last sermon for the year, I promise! That's pretty rash for January, isn't it?

Glad the trip to Lord Howe was successful for you, it is a special place. Imagine what it must have been like when Ruby and Bill went there for their honeymoon. Though it sounds as though Bill wasn't leaving too much to your imagination! Good on him, I say. Did you make any New Year's resolutions? I made Ruby's cake for afternoon tea one day when some friends from out of town dropped by. It didn't taste as wonderful as I remember hers, but it was still delicious. Thank you, and can you thank Bill too, for sharing the secret (?) family recipe? It means a lot.

Sat up one night and wrote this piece about Xmas ... not sure how it's working ... what do you think? Does it need more, or less, lemon?

Will be in touch again, soon. I send triple-strength wishes – that you may have a much gentler year this year than last –

Finn

Christmas?

'Tis the season of duty, going to parties where you plan how to get away before you even get there. Then you drink too little as others drink too much. They all look like peeled pig's balls but you can't let on, 'cause he's the boss and you're on a short contract, again. The food makes you think of the 1950s and long for something that looks like it once had something to do with the natural world. You realise that the shirt you bought in a hurry last Friday isn't pure cotton after all, but some sweat-inducing polyester. And when you're desperate to leave, the friend who offered to drive you home is groin-deep in chatting up.

There's that mad rush at work to finish all that has to be done before the year's end, or else. Or else what I don't know, but that's the pressure. So everyone acts two-faced, full of *bonhomie* and *have a nice Xmas*, at the same time roiling at inefficiencies which they think will make all the difference in that race to the start of the Holidays.

Then it's the holidays, where you try to unwind, but keep remembering things you should have done, slights contained in Xmas cards, and what *did* that fridge-side comment from the boss's secretary mean? The nightmares make you sweat even more than the polyester shirt. You find you've murdered a client or he's out to murder you, or both events run simultaneously in your personal horror movie, where you don't even have to drive-in, it drives in for you, all the way in.

If you're going away, it's the health anxieties. Is that lump really cancer? How to organise to get it checked and not let on to anyone? How to secure the house against flood, fire, cyclone, burglars, cat-murder and garden pillage all in two days? Are the new neighbours reliable citizens or pyromaniacs? Do the gutters really have to be cleaned? What about that leaning tower of gum tree? Would it survive a big blow?

It's the family phone calls. All cheer and *I love you* and *We're having a great day.* Followed by beery Boxing Day calls where *Something has to be done about Dad. He's become impossible* and *You don't know what it's like, you live so bloody far away* and *I'm gunna stick the whipper snipper up his arse if something isn't done about him soon.* The kids are all hungover. The parents feel equally yellow from too much grog in the middle of a tired day. There's the problem of how to fit all the wrapping paper in the recycle bin along with all the bottles, and where to store all the unwanted detritus Santa sent.

It's that lull before New Year's Eve. More futile, febrile shopping. Too many people walking off their disappointments and family violence in public spaces. The Xmas carols piped through the shopping centre raise homicidal tendencies as smoothly as snake charmers. Lunch at the fast foodery is distracted by the sight of a woman, waxy with loneliness. The eyes of those in contented company rake her melting chin till only a dribbly nub of candle is left to pick at her box of damp and twisted chips.

New Year's Eve is force-fed fun and cellophane optimism. Followed by the morning's stagger through the living room. There, lumpen bodies writhe on underclad mattresses, emerging as hairy-arsed men attempting witticisms over coffee. Suddenly a longing for the hermit's life overwhelms you. There are only two days left to clean up the house and yard. Then it's back to work. To greet a New Year that feels about as new as an orphan's teddy bear. And we start all over again the year long, grinding cycle — leading to the glittering prize of the Annual Christmas Holiday.

January 17

Dear Finn

Well we made it safely home, and found everything in order here. Those bushfires hadn't come near the place. I think if the house burnt down now I'd burn down myself.

The big news is that Leigh's results have come out, and she did well enough to get into the Uni course she wanted – celebrations all round! I feel proud of her, managing to do well under rough conditions. Guess, as you say, our daughters are made of tough stuff. No, I'm not going to take any of the credit for her achievements, but I can't help feeling that we might have had a bit to do with providing the right kind of loving. So many people have cake-shops full of talent, but poverty or violence or other forms of terror thwart them, don't they? How I grieve to see all their cakes grow mildew, or shrivel into perverse and bitter biscuits, often poisoning the next generation.

Leigh is thinking of seeing if her place in the course can be deferred to the beginning of next year though. Many late-night discussions, as you can imagine. It might be wise but ... not obviously so! She says she'd like to take a year off, so she can do some growing up without the pressure to perform all the time. I can see her point, and especially after a year like the last. She wants to move up to Brisbane, get a part-time job and just have some space to herself. Of course what I haven't mentioned yet is that she met this boy on Lord Howe Island, she thinks he's rather gorgeous. And, you guessed it, he's studying at University of Queensland. Hmmm. I didn't see a lot of him, but what I did see seemed classy and highly appealing, if you like that kind of slick-muscled, young male thing. I don't! Maybe just a bit too perfect and cocksure for my liking. Only saw him a couple of times, they tended to rendezvous on the beach rather than at our apartment, but my gut didn't like him. He was always so slimy polite to me. Leigh reckons I'm just being super-sensitive, that I'm programmed to suspect any boy who's interested in her, but I'm not so sure. Maybe she's right and I'm just feeling ultra-cautious after all the traumas of the past year. But, if there's one lesson I've learned over the years, it's to trust my gut. Apart from any of that, I have severe doubts about the idea of her moving cities for a bloke she barely knows, but she swears that's not the sole reason. Like Lola she can argue such a watertight case, and cites you as someone who took time out from formal education without coming to a bad end. I'm struggling with these contradictions. But at this stage struggling, not going under, you'll be pleased to know. Ania and Bill both support Leigh's plot, but are being careful not to paint me as the ogre who says 'No'. You took a year or two off between school and uni. Was that useful? What do you think, or better still, advise?

All my clients were pleased to see me back on deck. Christmas is hard to survive for most of them. I feel much less shaky most days and think I'm doing strong work with them. I now have a greater insight into the effects of trauma and grief than I did before – isn't that a surprise? The nurse who'd been working in a refugee camp, I think I mentioned her to you once, is making progress, thanks to her own potent desire to re-connect with life, but also, I think, because I now understand a little more of what she experienced. I'm never, NEVER going to say that Ruby's death was useful or a good thing or any of those other silver-lining bloody cliches, but I guess I have to say that in terms of my informal education, I've just lumbered my way up one of the steepest learning curves. What was it you wrote about having a PhD in grief?

Not sure how I feel about your description of Christmas, especially as this last one was a strong, positive family time for me. But there are millions of people (and a large percentage of my clients would agree) whose Annual Christmas Holidays sound just as futile and unrefreshing as you describe. Perhaps more lemon rather than less. I love your sharp tongue, maybe because my own has become so mild and soft from all the years of licking Ania's sweet flesh! Not! It'll be pretty weird for us if Leigh leaves the house this year. It'd be the first time ever in our relationship living by ourselves, able to do as we please. Maybe we'll install a waterbed!

As you can see from this, I'm in a much better space than I have been for a while, though I'm not silly enough to think that it will stay that way. Hope this finds you plump and content –

Love to you all – Molly.

Dear Molly,

Far from plump and content, life here is somewhat thin and deranged. They've decided to close down my department. I no longer have a job, as of next Wednesday! There have been rumours flying around for some months but I didn't want to pass them on. Thought you had other more pressing matters to preoccupy you, and they were just rumours at that stage. The boss kept an optimistic front, always hopeful that some semblance of rationality would descend upon the economic rationalists currently running the university. He couldn't believe that they could believe in a university without a Department of History. But his optimism proved wrong. Those at the top left it until really late, to see how enrolments in History subjects were going in the New Year, met last Thursday, looked at the figures, decided that the whole department was no longer viable and sent round a memo cancelling all our courses ... not to mention our livelihoods! To say I feel shocked doesn't begin to tell the story.

We have to vacate our offices by next week. And no-one has mentioned the possible fate of all our post-graduates. Or what happens to all the undergraduates who were majoring in History, a lot of them planning to become history teachers in High Schools. But where do they go now? Because we're so isolated, it's not like they can stay in the same city and transfer across to a different university to continue with their specialisation. Whenever I go into work I find splatters of desperate students wanting to know the answers to such questions, needing academic counselling, but I don't know any of the answers and feel in need of some counselling myself!

The union isn't able to help much, though they're doing their darnedest to negotiate decent redundancy packages for all of us. Of course, a large sum of money would be great, but for me there's so much more to working than just the money. Remember how excited I was when I got tenure the year before last? That was a big joke, huh? Like a dolt, I let myself be lulled into a dream of things being reliable and plannable for a little while ... but I knew at 16, I knew that the only certainty in the world was uncertainty, there was no such thing as security. How could I be so stupid as to forget that? My mum's sudden death, and Ruby's more recently, should have strengthened my sense that dramatic change is the most likely thing in store for us ... but no, I had to bury my stupid head in a riff of mangoes and babies and satisfied students and peace in suburbia. Could give myself a hard shake for being so ... whatever.

It's particularly hard because I feel so powerless. There is nothing I, or any of my colleagues, can do. The economic rationalists are irrational. They have their ears stoppered against anything other than profit and loss arguments, so representations from us are useless. Just like with the old bastard who used to molest me ... protests about ordinary, simple human needs are pointless. Guess that's why the sudden feeling of being powerless has knocked me so far out of the garden of contentment.

Angus has been very supportive. And I'm grateful that at least we'll still have his income to be going on with. Though his contract finishes in about twelve months time and there's no predicting whether it'll be renewed. Silly little details like merit and dedication are totally irrelevant nowadays. I've never been economically dependent on him before. He says of course I can trust him, but I'm itchy with a rash of "what if"s. And now I have no choice. No choice at all.

Didn't want to burden you with this when you're just regaining some equilibrium. But it's not some minor event that I could keep quiet about and then drop into the conversation casually, six months down the track. Maybe we can keep each other up to date with our varying degrees of vertigo as we stagger up our respective learning curves. I'm not suggesting that what's happened to me in any way equates with your mum's death. I don't see them being at all comparable on the Richter scale of life-changing events. But I do feel incredibly discombobulated, as Ruby used to say. Suddenly realise I've never been unemployed before. Guess that makes me one of the very lucky ones, but it sure is a strange feeling after so many years to find myself out on the cliff-edge, with all this freedom and time available. It's something I used to dream of achieving one day, but not this way. Maybe once I get over feeling shaken, resentful, tiny-girl powerless, furious, indignant, hurt, dismayed and generally shocked ... maybe I'll be able to get some pleasure out of this change. Right now I can't, quite.

Other news. Lola's back at school, having had a pretty wobbly first few days. She loves her teacher but a lot of her best friends have moved to a new school closer to their home suburbs. So there are daily fluctuations in who she sits near, who won't talk to her, who's going to be her friend forever, and so on. It's all so intense at that age, isn't it? And again I feel powerless to do anything about it, except listen and give her cuddles at the end of each day.

What has Leigh decided to do? Like you, I can see arguments both ways, but basically if she doesn't feel ready to start uni, then I'd say she shouldn't. I've seen too many people struggling through their first year as if they were wading in sludge, simply because they weren't ready to be there. Much better to take some time out and muck around for a bit, especially given what she's just been through. Yes, I did take a year off between school and uni but out of necessity. My circumstances were very different to Leigh's. Think she should rest up if she wants to. My bet is she'll be thoroughly bored by May, and then she can either work hard and save money so she doesn't have to work part-time in her first year, or she may be able to enrol mid-year. Is she planning to live with Bill, if she moves up to Brisbane? Would be great company for him, I imagine, but the emergence of her nascent sexuality with island lover-boy could be cramped by having Grandpa pottering round outside the bedroom door!

In spite of all the other stuff happening, I have to say, it was as satisfying as eating chocolate cake, reading your last letter. You sounded so much less fragmented. I'm truly impressed with your capacity to heal fast and hold firm to the solid bits of your life. How's the jelly woman? I think you're wise to expect that she'll be a regular companion for some time to come. Angus and I loved your descriptions of letting her riot on Saturday mornings — accompanied by the sounds of doors slamming as Leigh and Ania moved sensibly out of range.

Will away to post this. Now at last I may be able to become one of those ideal mummies Lola and Leigh have both yearned for, you know the ones who pick their kids up at three every single day? You'd better watch out, next time you come up I might even have learnt how to bake biscuits. Remember those Peanut Butter Cookies I made once? They rattled round in the compost like hunks of shale for two years after the baking, or should I say, burning! Perhaps not biscuit baking.

Love to you — Finn

February 19

Dearest Finn

Saw this card a few weeks ago and bought it to slap on my fridge door ... 'cause there've been days when I really needed its command to 'NEVER GIVE UP'. But it sounds like you could do with it on your fridge door right now, you poor thing. I sort of couldn't believe your news. It just sounds so incredibly stupid. Such a waste of resources! And surely it can't do the university's reputation much good to close down such a vital dept, and with so little warning to the enrolled students? Not that I'm wasting any sympathy on the Uni – but to sack someone like you! When you've given so much to the job, and by anyone's standards were doing great work, in my totally unbiased opinion. Idiots!

Can understand how shocked you must feel. Listen, Leigh has decided to move to Brisbane, she leaves next week (down, Panic, down!) ... so we'll have a spare bedroom, if you need to come down here for a change of scene. That may be not the most obvious thing to do, what with money being tight and Lola and Angus to think of, but if it would help, you know I'd love it. We could lie out in the back yard and talk and drink. Sometimes when odd things happen, the only response is to act oddly yourself! That's my current motto ... it excuses my every eccentricity. Will talk with you soon, but in the meantime listen to the wild girl on the card.

Love you, always, Molly.

February 22

Dear Finn

Did the 'NEVER GIVE UP' girl get to you? After I put it in the post box I suddenly panicked with doubt about whether I'd put a stamp on it. My menopausal memory! At least that's my latest theory about my memory.

I've been thinking of you and wondering whether the shock of being sacked has gotten any smaller. Can imagine you waking up and automatically starting to plan your day's work and then being face-slapped by the realisation that you don't have any work to go to. Has that happened? After years of a routine, it's hard to shift out of it, even if it was a routine that you resented at times. Remember when Janet Frame talks about how she missed the label of 'incurable schizophrenic' after she finally received an accurate diagnosis? Although she'd hated and feared the label, it had been a big part of her identity for nearly ten years and when it was gone she felt both enormously relieved and frighteningly naked. Is that something like what you're feeling?

One issue you'll have to put your creative mind to work on quickly, is what to call yourself when people ask you what you do. Remember we discussed the language I feel comfortable using for my work, and you said then how important it was to get the words right? What about saying you're a writer? That covers a big range of possibilities, doesn't it? And it's accurate in terms of the past few years. How many books and articles have you published? And I can see it being even more so in the future. With Lola at school and lovely clear work-free days, you'll be able to write all those books you've had queuing up for attention, the ones you haven't been able to get to because of all the bumph at work. Or am I being too radically optimistic? Or just too cheerful, too early, about this major change you have to get used to?

The major news here is that Leigh's left for Brisbane. She's left home. We put her and several boxes of gear on the train at Central a couple of days ago. Dear god, it was hard to do. Ania took me out to dinner afterwards, to one of our favourite Vietnamese restaurants, but it wasn't much use. I kept being overtaken by big messy sobs. Couldn't even eat the chao tom (you remember, those prawns on sugar cane sticks?), and you know how much I love those. Ania drove me steadily home up the dark mountains, for which I am grateful. It would have been a total hazard to let this jelly woman drive, she doesn't even have a licence! Had to work the next day and I wasn't sure if I was going to be able to hold it together through the five appointments. Luckily one of them cancelled and I just scrabbled through. In some ways it was useful to have other people's dilemmas to focus on, otherwise the jelly woman would have had a field-day maundering on about losing both a mother and a daughter so close together. I know I haven't 'lost' Leigh in the same way that I've lost Ruby. At least I know that in my head. But the two events happening so close together does tend to spotlight their similarities to my undiscerning heart. And I am grieving for the end of that particular, intimate, nineteen-year relationship which has been Leigh and me up till now. Whatever comes next between us, and lots of it will be great, will be really different. Anyway, as you might guess, the jelly woman has increased her demands for time and space, and Ania and I are trying to accommodate her.

The good news is that Leigh arrived safely. She wasn't abducted by white slavers at Casino as the jelly woman predicted at three in the morning. She's staying with Bill for a while until she finds work, and then when she has some idea of her money she'll look round for a place of her own for the rest of the year. And she was able to defer her university place without drama. Gather she's been in contact with young Mr Slime and they've got a date lined up for this weekend. Dear god, I hope my gut is wrong about him. Just couldn't bear for anything more awful to happen now, especially to Leigh. If I look at it coolly it all sounds pretty fine, I guess, for a young woman her age. Guess I'll adjust eventually ... and you'll be pleased to hear I don't breathe a word of it to her!

Did feel for you when you talked about that feeling of powerlessness. Feel a bit that way myself about Leigh and the direction she's taking in her life. It's one of the biggest paradoxes of motherhood, isn't it? On the one hand you're incredibly powerful in terms of growing and feeding the child – such a complex and intricate task. But then there are times, like with the schoolyard politics you describe, when you feel completely helpless. Though I'm sure that all your cuddles and listening and discussions about coping strategies do help, significantly. But it doesn't feel nearly as good as the fantasy of swooping into the schoolyard like a Valkyrie and meting out violent justice to those who attack your baby, does it?

The night after Leigh left, I lunged into bed very early and Ania brought the mail in to me. In it was a book of poetry, sent by a friend who'd only just heard about Ruby. I flipped through it but was in no mood to read anything more complex than the pattern on my pillowcase. But the day after, I sat down with a pot of coffee and read it more thoughtfully. And found this piece which I just loved ... and thought you might like to apply, poultice-like, to your wounded psyche ... especially given what you said about feeling powerless. Do hope you like it. Best go now, I promised I'd do the grocery shopping before Ania got home this afternoon, and it's already quarter-past-four. See how you tempt me?

Remember how well loved you are, always

Molly.

the four men behind her

are playing poker / there's a soft whsk-whsk as they deal the cards /
*a woman alone at night / bad things happen to a woman like that /
yeah, that kind of woman is askin' for it / just askin' for it /* the men
lay out horrors with each hand / wanda beach / truro / anita cobby
/ a full house dealt face-up and screaming / she concentrates on
the defaced sign in front of her / *plain clot s and un formed lice
patrol this train /* the man with the ace of spades in the hole wins,
cuts the cards / wherever he cuts there's a queen / spades / dia-
monds / clubs / hearts / she reads the fine print / *in case of trouble
inform the guard /* there's a wisp of lint on his blue shirt sleeve / be
reasonable, luv / I can't stop people talking on the train / she retreats
to a corner seat / three women hear / one hums a blues riff under
her breath and they all get up / they find the carriage with the poker
players / the humming woman croons a single note / her friends
harmonise / they serenade the men in faultless *a cappella* / they
sing the *menstruation blues* / at the first mention of blood the men
abandon their cards / they prise the doors open and / leap out of
the train / even though it's still / moving /

Dear Molly,

Yes, the never give up girl made it safely home, and has taken up residence on the fridge door. Some days I argue with her, and ask 'Why not?' but she shows the greatest disinterest in such feeble queries and just keeps on jumping (or is it stamping?) gleefully on apathy and other such signs of inanity. Yes, you're right about the adoption of an occupation label, though at present only bitter ones spring round my head like hyperactive gymnasts ... what about 'redundant teacher of irrelevant information about past lives', or 'independent researcher into the history of elderly underwear', or when I feel like a complete oxymoron, 'unemployed housewife'. I take your point about seeing the positive side of all this clear space, and I can imagine that one day I will. Right now though, I'm in the midst of missing my students, trying to help the abandoned PhD students I *was* supervising to sort out the next bit of their lives, fighting with myself about graciously accepting that I'll have to be economically dependent on Angus for a while, trying to negotiate the redundancy package arrangements, setting up a complete home office without spending all my savings (I'll need to get a fax and laser printer if I'm going to work from home as a writer, I think), avoiding the use of Angus and Lola as dumpsters for my free-floating rage, and other such petty tasks. There are a few weary miles to go before I can start feeling optimistic and enthusiastic about this. None of the projects in the queue interest me as much as lying on the bed and looking at the mould and spider-webs patterning the ceiling. Maybe a few more weeks. Maybe I need to invite your jelly woman up here and have a few riotous sessions wailing and drinking whisky and then I might get round to discovering I'm inspired about something.

Sorry — feel I'm the one who should be writing cheerful letters to you, instead of maundering on bitterly. Really don't love myself and my current mood very much. How's Leigh going in Brisbane now? Did the date with lover-boy work out? I hope her instincts and not yours are right about him. And Bill? Can't imagine wanting to stay with my grandfather at nineteen but then again Bill isn't your average Grandpa either. Do hope they're getting on okay.

One thing I did like, was the menstruation blues poem you sent, made me laugh out loud. Thanks. I've taped it above my desk so that whenever I sit there nervelessly trying to sort out the mess, I can read it and hum encouragingly to myself. Do wish you were here to whiz up a jug of mango daiquiris and sing inebriated blues with me on some of these endless muggy afternoons. I miss you too much. Think I have to go and lie down or Lola and Angus will come home to mopey me, again.

Talk to you soon, sorry for being such a sour-sop, love you –

Finn

March 21

Dear Finn

You asked for news of Leigh and her island romance hero.
Well, there's certainly a tale to tell. She went on that date
the weekend after she got to Brisbane. And it was cool.
They went out a couple of times after that, to the movies
once, to a pub gig another time. Then last weekend he
invited her out to dinner and she said yes. Had a lovely
time getting ready, Grandpa let her borrow Ruby's antique
amber necklace, and they both thought she looked pretty
stunning as she set out. Can you remember the breathless
pleasure of preparing for a first dinner date? Well,
apparently the dinner was fine, Kevin was attentive and
courteous, held hands across the table while they waited
for dessert. Then there was some chat about who'd pay for
the meal, and he said he'd pay for this one and when
Leigh got her first pay, she could take him out. Leigh
thought this was fine, feeling pretty pleased at the
implication that he saw them as a long-term item.

Anyway they drove back to his college, Leigh imagining
that they'd have a cup of coffee and maybe do some
kissing and then he'd drive her home. But when they got
back to his room he put the hard word on her, straight up.
She said she wanted to slow down a bit and he got really
shirty. Asked her what she was saving it for. She tried to
move out of his embrace and he wouldn't let her go. At
this point she was getting pretty worried. Then someone
knocked on his door and he did let her go, while he went
to open it. She grabbed her bag and made ready for a
quick exit. At the door were three of his college mates, all
really pissed. She smelt serious danger. They asked Mr
Slime what he was up to and he told them he was just
trying to persuade the little bitch to give up her virginity,

there wasn't any point hanging onto it, was there? They all laughed and said they'd love to give him a hand. One of them grabbed her, put his arm round her waist, sleazed his groin against her leg and, laughing down into her face, said he had some pretty effective tools of persuasion if she cared for a sample. At this point Leigh's worry became desperation.

Thinking fast, she laughed back and said, 'Maybe. You reckon yours is better than Kevin's? I'd love to check that out. But right now I'm busting for a piss. Where's the loo, guys?' Kevin was reluctant to let her go, but after she'd appealed to the other blokes that all she wanted to do was have a leak and then come back for some fun, he gave her directions. As soon as she got out the door she bolted as nonchalantly as she could. When she was out of sight she whipped the mobile out of her bag, hurrying madly down the corridors all the while, desperately trying to find a way out of the building. She called Bill and asked him to pick her up outside the college porter's office. After a few terrifying minutes of feeling completely lost she got outside, worked out which road they'd driven in on, and made her way to the well-lit porter's office. Her skin crept at every noise, she kept thinking they were coming after her. Said it was the longest twenty-five minutes. Thought she was going to wet herself, she really did need a piss, but hadn't wanted to waste time going to the toilet in case Kevin and his mates came after her. She was so terrified that they'd find her and somehow drag her back to that room.

When she rang me, after she was safely home with Bill (bless him for being at home and awake!) and he'd made her some hot milk, she sounded so small, like a betrayed preschooler. I wanted to get on the next plane and wrap her up in eiderdowns forever. We talked for ages and she was going to take half a sleeping tablet in order to try to get some sleep. Bill had a few on hand. After she and I had talked, Bill came on the phone sounding furious, ready to inflict the most vicious tortures on Kevin! I felt much the same, but just so grateful that Leigh had the wit to get out of there before ... As you can imagine I didn't get much sleep that night, and there weren't any sleeping potions handy here. My whole being cried out to take some action, but I couldn't think what to do. In the eyes of the world 'nothing happened', nothing that is, except the crushing of a young woman's excitement about exploring her sexuality, her trust in men, her joy in launching out into the world as a fresh person with lots to offer, her willingness to love openly ... all that ... crushed because a few privileged young pricks were bored and wanted a bit of excitement on a Saturday night, and there's nothing quite like gang banging a virgin to top off a good night's drinking, is there?

Of course, Bill and I are really worried about Kevin trying to track Leigh down. Loss of face in front of your mates is something which would need to be avenged in his system of logic, I'd say. He knows where Leigh's living, he picked her up from Bill's place that night ... Leigh had been careful not to give him her address on the first few dates, but thought it was OK with this one because he seemed so nice! Leigh and Bill are trying to make sure she's not in the house alone too much. I feel scared for her and rake myself with doubt, wondering whether there was anything I could have done to prevent this. My gut was right but there's no comfort in being able to say, 'I told you so'. Leigh has to trust other people sometimes — or else live like a paranoid snail. I'm just so thankful that she thought fast and smart. And had the courage to act instead of being paralysed by the brutal power of that room full of leering boys. And that she had the mobile, and that it was working. Keep imagining the 'what ifs'. My biggest anxiety is that she'll become inert with fear, especially with this happening so soon after Ruby's freaky accident. It wouldn't be totally crazy for her to see a rapist and a fatal car accident on every corner, with all these events crashing into one another in her short life. Should I suggest she sees a counsellor, or is that likely to sound too much like interference? The spectre of the 'over-protective' mother haunts me. And yet, I feel ... maybe I could have done something more to protect her from this. Shit.

Feel flattened. I'm running very low on hope, and any faith I had in something good being round the next corner is worn thin as a silver-eye's ankle bone. Do you think I could employ you to perform as my modern-day Scheherezade? Remember she told stories each night to keep the Sultan Shariah entertained and happily distracted? Do you think you could find some stories to tell me, to distract me ... will it go on like this forever?

Hope you're OK. I get constant anxiety attacks about all my loved ones, imagining that dire things are happening to them whenever they're out of sight. Ania's administrator is absolutely sick of me ringing her to see if Ania's all right. Please send me something that might help to calm me, I feel like I'm drowning again.

Love from Molly.

Dear Molly,

One good thing about being unemployed, I can reply to your letters pronto. Not that I would've waited long to reply to this one anyway. It was so disturbing — and the bloody injustice of it. I'm with Bill, red-hot scalpel at the ready to inflict the bloodiest torture on young Kevin's tenderest parts. Pack of bastards. Those wealthy college boys are a law unto themselves, aren't they? Think the world's there for them to pick the eyes out of. And they get away with so much. Leigh was very smart, and very lucky. I do feel for her. I'm incredibly glad she doesn't have any physical wounds to heal — thanks to her clear-thinking strength and your sensible gift of the mobile phone — but the internal wounds to her sense of trust and, as you say, her pleasure in being a beautiful, fresh-to-life, young woman ... they'll take some time and care to repair.

Can understand your reticence about suggesting a counsellor, but what about reminding her of the success she had in going to the Women's Health Centre before? That wouldn't be giving her advice, so much as reminding her of her own effective strategy, which she used last time she was in strife. I'm sure there would be similar set-ups in Brisbane. I could ask one of my friends there if she knows of a particularly good one, if you like.

Not sure about being your Scheherezade ... she was an incredibly talented storyteller, wasn't she? And 1001 nights is an awful long time! Do you know, Lola loves that book, we had to read it, cover to cover just recently? One thing I will share with you though, is a Cherokee Indian curse. I just love the clear, deadly focus of the words ... perhaps you and Leigh could make one up with Mr Slime in mind? May all his meals be too hot and the inside of his mouth be coated in blisters for the rest of his life. That might be a start. Here's the curse:

Careful: my knife drills your soul
Listen, whatever-your-name-is
        one of the wolf people
listen   I'll grind your saliva into the earth
listen   I'll cover your bones with black flint
listen   I'll cover your bones with black feathers
listen   I'll cover your bones with black rocks
Because you are going where it's empty
        Black coffin on the hill
listen   the black earth will hide you, will
        find you a black hut
        out where it's dark, in that country
listen   I'm bringing a box for your bones
        a black box
        a grave with black pebbles
listen   your soul's spilling out
listen   it's blue

What do you reckon? If pointing the bone can work, why not a few well-honed and bony words? Can see Bill getting right into it, given his current mood.

Think you're right to worry about the bastard wanting to pursue Leigh. Embarrassed young men are more lethal than the proverbial scorned woman. But Bill can't mount a 24-hour watch on her and it wouldn't be healthy for either of them if he tried to. She got herself out of an extremely dangerous situation by using her brains and I think that's what she needs reminding of, constantly. It's the most reliable form of protection we have, I guess.

Writing to you about curses reminds me about the fate of one of my poems. A curious tale, of sorts. I published it in an obscure women's anthology and then heard that a rape crisis counsellor was using it in her 8-week healing

146

program for survivors of rape and incest. Apparently at the end of the course, each participant wrote the name of their particular torturer on a small piece of paper, placed the paper on a fire and watched it burn whilst loudly chanting my poem. She said it was a very effective ritual. Not sure what else she did in the course, but it sounded interesting. I'll enclose the poem, in case you want to pass it on to Leigh, and will try to think of something more distracting for you next time.

If money weren't so uncertain, I'd enclose a large denomination note and tell you in undeniably dictatorial fashion, to go and have an hour-long massage. You really need it, and I'm sure the jelly woman wouldn't be averse to such tender treatment. Can you organise it? I'm sure your panic would diminish under the hands of a caring masseur. And who knows, even your flattened soul might resurrect itself?

Is it my imagination or are we taking it in turn to play optimist for each other?

Will leave off there and muse on the idea of becoming your Scheherezade. Go and have that massage or I may never write to you again. I do love you. Please give my love to Leigh when next you talk, and tell her to ring me anytime she might want a loving voice to link onto.

Love you — Finn

i turn on you i burn you up

if it didn't hurt i'd pluck them
pluck my lips
bare my vicious vengeful grin
vagina dentata is an old fear
and yes
i like it
i want your foul old-man smell to be
the smell of fear
old man smell my fury
shut up for 20 years
now it's out
it smells ferocious

you were truly
the cliche
the worm in the bud
you horned your old-man's thumb into
soft and trusting
again and again

i kept silent
hate you became hate me
i tap into that hate
a tap of blood to wash you out
i bleed on you all over gouts and clots of darkest blood
thick to suffocate you drown slowly slowly you
can't grasp a breath it's thick and sweet this blood
like the caramels you tried to bribe
it gags you like me
you are kept silent

sweet silent blood sweet as the names you
called me your ray of sunshine
now you are a piece of old paper
i am a ray of the sun truly

i turn on you i burn you up

April 4

Dear Finn

Saw this card and it brought tears to my eyes. Reminded me of what you said about your mother and how irises reminded you of her and that reminded me of my mother ... if that makes any sense. Took your advice. I was in such a mess I'd have washed myself in kerosene if someone had said it'd make me feel less awful. Thankfully your advice was not that extreme. Found out the name of a masseur from Ania's long-suffering administrator, and since you wrote I've had two long sessions. They were, or are, heavenly. I come out feeling more relaxed than I have for, well, it must be over a year now. Why isn't there a therapeutic massage centre on every street corner? Maybe that will be my next radical crusade – to convert all the pubs in Australia into massage centres. Then instead of everyone trying to drink away their problems, they could just pop in and get someone to massage them away. Think of the money society would save. It'd be a real revolution, don't you reckon?

Thanks for sending me the poem. Can see it being effective in some therapy situations. Not sure about passing it on to Leigh, especially when I'm not there. I'll file it away and doubtless it'll be just the thing I need one day. Don't mean that to sound as ironic as it does.

Am running out of space. Just wanted you to know the massage miracle cure was proving to be just that. So any time you want to be my dictator, please go right ahead. Though I still can't help dreaming, and preferring, you in the role of Scheherezade. Must go, lots of love to Lola and Angus, and post-massage caresses to you. Wise friend.

Molly.

Dear Molly,

Thanks for the card, it brought tears to my eyes too ... maybe we should start a Motherless Daughters Society with an iris as its emblem? No, maybe we should just get together more often and indulge ourselves in everything we feel like. Now I have so much time available I find I miss your laughter and provocative talk a lot. Am slowly adjusting to living more slowly, though the question of money still gnaws at me at 3 a.m. And the redundancy deal is *still* not finalised. Feel like I'm skin-stitched on to the university until that's resolved, like I'll only be able to get on with working out what to do next once it's completed. Where are the scissors of simplicity when you need them most? What news of Ruby's life insurance arrangements? And I guess her estate isn't settled yet. Is it complicated?

Had a phone call from a woman the other day ... hadn't heard from her for fifteen years or so ... she'd come across some of my writing and was prompted by curiosity to track my whereabouts. We had a long chat, though I think she was a mite disappointed to learn of my domestic bliss and maternal status. Last time she caressed my breasts neither of us knew anything, and cared less, about the magnificent art of breast-feeding! But I get ahead of myself ... realised after her phone call that this was a chapter in my history which I'd kept completely secret from you ... partly because it happened when you were struggling, immersed in raising a tiny Leigh, and partly because I was on shaky ground ethically ... and felt embarrassed about that.

We met at a women's discussion group, and I saw her every fortnight for a year or so in that setting. We'd sort of flirt and tease one another, as you do when debating ideas sometimes, and I knew she was an out lesbian but that was all the friendship amounted to. Then one time in the group, we were discussing dancing, and I was lamenting the fact that I didn't go to nightclubs any more because I hated the macho, meat-market feeling. Katya (the woman in question) suggested that the discussion group's next event should be an outing to one of the all-women's clubs, for a night's dancing. There was general agreement to this idea and a date was set. Well, when I turned up in my best dancing tights, at the arranged time and place, there was no-one else there except Katya. Of course, we did the only logical thing and danced all night together ... and when we fell, laughing, out of the club at some early hour of the morning, Katya pulled me into this bus-shelter and kissed me ... and whenever I drive past that particular bus-shelter I experience a hot flush all over — one that has nothing to do with menopause.

She invited me back to her apartment. She said as we both had sore feet from dancing, we should have a footbath and she had some new bath oil which promised complete resuscitation of all aching body parts. She thought that now might be an excellent time to try it out. Well, I was still feeling pretty shaken by the sudden seismic shifts in our connection, so I agreed! Landed back at her Japanese style apartment and duly set about the gentle art of foot bathing ... though it turned out she had a bottle of very good malt whisky she needed me to try out too. With my feet being bathed and anointed by her able fingers and my brain being bathed and anointed by the equally agile whisky ... is it any wonder that I ended up staying in her apartment for the very brief remainder of the night? The heated towels she used to dry my fresh-washed feet were the final deciders ... I'd never been so skilfully seduced.

Have just looked at the clock, and realised that I'd better make like Cinderella and transform myself back into my ordinary motherly self or else I'll be late collecting Lola from swimming, and she hates that. Will write again soon, do let me know if you want to hear any more about this particular story which your Scheherezade suggestion and that unexpected phone call seduced me into telling. How are you enjoying having the house to yourselves?

love to you, and Ania, from Finn

April 28

Dear Finn

Getting your last letter was almost as good as a mango
daiquiri — and I really needed it. Do continue with the
tale of the mysterious Katya, I'm curious and a little
amazed at what you've kept hidden all these years, and
I really need distractions right now.

We took advantage of the Anzac long weekend and drove
up to Brisbane to visit Leigh and Bill. The drive up was fun,
Ania and I enjoyed driving long-distance mulling over miles
and miles of stories as you describe it, listening to all our
favourite tapes, and I was really looking forward to seeing
Leigh. But it turned out to be the hardest weekend. In my
eagerness to see Leigh I'd forgotten the impact of being in
Ruby's space when it's Ruby-less. The effect of her not
being there. I can't adjust.

Bill looked like a sad old black Labrador. Leigh like a
puppy that's just been beaten. Both of them have been
struggling to put on a brave face for each other but as soon
as we arrived the grief pushed through. Bill cooked a huge
roast to celebrate our arrival but when Ania went in to offer
last minute assistance with serving, she found him in tears
over the gravy. That had always been Ruby's special skill ...
making the world's best gravy. We had the roast without,
and no one commented on the somewhat woody potatoes.
Poor Dad. He's really worried about Leigh too, and is
finding all the administrative crap and intrusive questions
relating to Ruby's life insurance disturbing. Do you know
one investigator asked him whether Ruby had been
depressed and expressing suicidal thoughts recently?
As if she might have hired someone to drive up onto the
pavement to kill her! Bill was incredibly upset by that ...

153

it was just a routine question according to the investigator ... but what a question!

And Leigh ... I can hardly write about her ... the wrench of waving goodbye to her ... to drive a thousand kilometres away when she's so .... it's one of the hardest things I've ever done. Of course we suggested she come home with us, even for a short stay, but she feels she needs to grow out on her own and says she doesn't want to give in to her desire to sook back home, as she put it. Apparently she has an appointment to see a counsellor at the Women's Centre in Bill's suburb next week, which gives me some comfort. I just hope she gets lucky and strikes a good one. She's finding it very hard to go out by herself. She stays in bed till midday most days, watches the entire afternoon's worth of soaps, then cooks dinner for her and Bill. Then they watch a bit of TV together and go to their respective beds. It's not much of a life for a nineteen-year-old, is it? But as Ania says, maybe just stopping still in a safe place is the best way for Leigh to get back to strength and recover from the shocks she's had. Maybe – I just hope it's not the onset of major depression ... that's what I feared most last year ... and she'd only just dug herself out of that when all this had to happen. It's so damn unfair.

I tried to give her lots of TLC and support and kept reminding her of how cleverly she handled the dangers of Kevin and his mates ... but I left feeling helpless. What are a few words and hugs when she feels so betrayed and afraid? Ania had to do most of the driving on the way back as I was pretty much a total jelly woman – again. We laughed, in a desperate way, about her driving me, sobbing, down the highways of life. I must say I feel bloody lucky to have her by me right now.

As you can imagine, I felt bleak and listless when we got home. And I seem to swing between a blancmange of apathy ... like 'what's the point of anything?', interspersed with vindaloo rages over the most unlikely things. For instance, we watched the news the night we got home (think Ania wanted to blank out a bit) and there was footage of the Anzac Day marches, with the usual array of sad, doddery diggers, crumpling under the weight of all those polished medals. Well the sight of them threw me headfirst into a fury about why they should still be alive when Ruby was dead. What did they have to live for? What could they offer society? ... and so on and on. Poor Ania retreated out the back for a well-earned glass of wine and left me to it. And quite right too. I felt so ashamed afterwards, it was completely irrational, not to mention unfair and unprovoked ... but there was no resisting it at the time ... it just flung out. Is this grief, or menopause, or madness, or a brutal combination of all three? I came very close to smashing the television. Really wanted to smash something and feel it break under my fists. Not sure what to do, maybe I should look up some of my psych texts on grief, but from memory they provide lists of symptoms in neat stages, and chronicle their order ... and there's nothing orderly about these feelings ... they hurl me about like birth contractions.

Please write soon, I need your words even more than usual. Hope things are better at your end of the continent –

Love always – Molly.

My poor Molly,

How I understood your letter. Can remember feeling just those pummelling rages after my mother died. And all those questions — as if death could be bothered with something as puny as logic, as if some simple code of fairness might govern it. But knowing that the raging questions are fruitless is part of the problem isn't it? I found swimming helped sometimes, smashing my arms through the water as if it were the source of all injustice. Another friend had a rolled-up futon mattress in her living room and whenever she felt one of those momentous rages, she'd put on loud rock music and kick the bejesus out of the futon ... the music helped to muffle the sound of the blows and the accompaniment of growls and yells she let loose with her kicks. Anything's worth a try ... just remember not to flail out at hard objects or you'll break your hand ... and that's excruciating.

The weekend excursion sounded utterly miserable ... meals eaten through the glaze of grief are truly horrible. The food somehow tastes as if tears and orphans' handkerchiefs are the prime ingredients, no matter what it's really made of. Your description of Bill's roast ... I could feel one of the lumps of undercooked potato in my throat for hours after I'd finished reading it. Poor all of you. I could say that it gets a bit less awful as time passes, and I'd be telling you the truth ... but I know from sour experience how useless that sounds when you're right in the middle of a haemorrhage. But the bleeding amputated feeling does diminish ... I swear on the muscle of our friendship that this does happen ... even though I know it seems impossible for you to believe right now.

You are palpably not in your usual mode of commanding life ... but I'll continue with Katya's story anyway, imagining that I'm following your orders.

Well after the night of the long footbaths, I crept home round midday ... fortunately Angus was away ... so I had time to reflect, at leisure, on the events, moral iniquities and serious pleasures of the previous evening. Katya was a persuasive and persistent lover, and having known me for some time she knew a lot of my weaknesses ... so I'd resolve not to see her again and then she'd ring to say she had tickets to a concert which she knew I'd been desperate to see and we'd go and then afterwards we'd find ourselves back at her apartment sampling a different malt whisky and a different set of her expensive sheets, and I'd turn up to work the next day in the previous day's clothes, hoping no-one would notice the rumpled, I-haven't-slept look ... I was heading down the path towards major liver and moral collapse. But having such luscious fun!

At this stage I hadn't mentioned any of these events to Angus, as you might imagine. Sounds a bit pathetic but I felt incredibly confused, and I didn't want to hurt either Angus or Katya. The idiotic, unforgivable logic of the two-timer! Well of course, one balmy night they met at a function and Angus, territorial instincts roused, guessed. As soon as we left he asked me bluntly if anything was happening between Katya and me. Well, I'm a hopeless liar, so I told him the truth.

There followed some very hectic months. I sometimes floated myself above it and thought it sounded too ridiculous even as the plot of a soap opera. But that didn't stop it being my situation. Katya and I had a great relationship while we were in her bed, but elsewhere we didn't always get on, as might be expected ... and when the going got tough her solution was to walk me back to the bedroom ... we could never discuss anything ... tongue-kissing and talking simultaneously was not a skill my mother taught me! Katya wanted me to leave Angus and move in with her ... and I was very tempted ... but beneath the undeniable erotic charge there were some murky power dynamics and I wasn't persuaded that we had enough clear-flowing integrity (I think that's the best word) between us to sustain a long deep friendship ... of the kind I already had going with Angus. I make it sound very clear-cut, as if there was always only going to be one solution, but that's certainly not how it felt in the middle of it. I had the worst case of emotional vacillation known to womankind, and I knew I was hurting both of them badly. They both saw me as being in the most powerful position, having it both ways on easy street ... and I could see how they could see that ... but it felt very different. My feminist friends thought life with Katya would be best, and some days when we'd laugh and stroke each other all languid afternoon, I thought the same. It was strange being in bed with someone who was very much smaller than me ... made me feel large, strong and protective toward Katya ... even though she made it clear she didn't need protection from anyone. But then there was my history with Angus. He'd supported me through some gritty times and we could talk so easily. Very different minds but they liked each other, sparked off each other, and after a night arguing about philosophies over a bottle of red wine, and then falling into bed for some very amicable, almost reverent sex ... well I'd feel that life with Angus was the way to go. And so it went on for some time ...

But I'd better stop lolling about playing your Scheherezade, dust off my university face and latch it in place, because I have a meeting in half-an-hour, to finalise the redundancy package. Fingers crossed.

So, keep on paddling and resting, paddling and resting, it's the only technique I know for surviving the rough straits of grief. I'll write again as soon as I can,

love to you
always from Finn

PS Thought you might like this recipe. It's one of my favourites when I'm really miserable, and with the weather getting cooler down your way, it'd be especially good to eat beside the fire one night when you're in need of a Finn's comfort. Also it's incredibly easy to make.

Golden Syrup Self-saucing Pudding

Pudding:

4 tablespoons butter, melted
$^1/_2$ cup of sugar
1 cup of self-raising flour
$^1/_2$ cup of milk
$^1/_2$ teaspoon of vanilla essence
1 egg

Combine all dry ingredients in one large, deep, ovenproof bowl. Add melted butter. Then add lightly beaten egg, milk and vanilla, stirring vigorously for 2 minutes.

Sauce:

2 tablespoons of golden syrup
$1^1/_2$ cups of boiling water

Place golden syrup in heatproof measuring jug. Add boiling water. Mix till syrup dissolves. Pour on top of pudding mixture. Place in oven.

Cook in moderate, preheated oven (180°C) for 30–40 mins. (It takes a bit longer than this in my dodgy old oven ... but basically the cake mixture should be golden and firm to the touch and there should be a gooey rich sauce at the bottom of the dish.)

PPS And this — for obvious reasons ...

In Katya's Room ...

with ceremony she removes my clothes
drapes them on the side of her antique full-length stand-alone mirror
considers my body with connoisseur eye
elegant hands outline the plump she longs to drape round my hip/rib ridges

dropping the art-lover's pose
she pushes me
onto the bed
shows me her lover-arts
urgent small-finger force
dipping sliding etching
raising heat and nipples as she works
mouths meet and know just how to
mesh bite feed
air is scarce
moisture ascendant
smoothing coating
we are slick fast
holding melding
work of art working

finished ...

no, not quite
some hours
mapping murmuring lipping yet
some moments
lying close as earth and rock
idly asking ... was that vanilla?
a rough-sea-swim ... ripe brie ... surf-cold beer ...
thunderstorm dancing?
when we spool off the bed
to consider the world outside
we look in the antique full-length stand-alone mirror
we look pleasure-plump and different ...

in Katya's room.

May 18

Dear Finn

Great to get your word poultice – with all its added extras.
On the strength of it I gave myself the afternoon off last
Friday and, inspired by your recipe, prepared a special
meal for Ania. She's been such a lifesaver for me lately,
thought it was about time I got out of my apathy and did
something active about showing her that I do appreciate it.
That's something it does seem worth bothering about. One
of the worst things about Ruby's death is the sense that
I didn't ever tell her how important she was, how much
I loved the way she lived her life and how, although she
mothered differently, I thought she'd been a successful
mum in every sense that counts. All sounds pretty cliched
when I write it out like that, but it's what I wished I could
have said or written to her sometime. But now she's not
there – and I can't. Somehow I kidded myself that she'd
always be there, she was so strong and invincible,
I thought. I want to make damn sure that if Ania suddenly
dies on me, she knows what there is to know.

So I spent the afternoon listening to music (it's a big solace
at present) and cooking up a large pot of chicken tagine,
one of Ania's favourites. When Ania came home from a
pretty tense week at school, I poured her a large gin and
tonic, took her shoes off, gave her a footbath, then I dried
her slender, pale feet. Your friend Katya had some neat
ideas about pampering, didn't she? We ate the tagine with
cous-cous, sitting on the floor in front of the fire. Then after
we'd lazily sipped wine and chatted for a while, I popped
into the kitchen and whipped up your pudding. It looked
truly bizarre in the bowl, and I had my doubts as I put it in
the oven, but when I went back to check on it, voila, a
scrummy looking pudding that even Dame Pattie Menzies

would have been proud to present. We both had a large serving, accompanied by scoops of the best vanilla ice cream and then just lolled, feeling extremely wealthy. I read Ania your poem, which we both enjoyed ... can't believe you've kept this affair secret all these years. After all our indulgence, waddling to bed was the most difficult part of the evening, but once we got there I felt pretty close to serenity ... and it's been a long time since that feeling came anywhere near me.

Slept well, and although the jelly woman had been strictly banished from Friday night's dinner she wasn't too uppity in her demands on Saturday morning. Maybe, just maybe, she's becoming more manageable. What did you say about time?

Had a long talk on the phone with Leigh on the weekend too. She quite liked the counsellor she saw, and is going to do a volunteer's training course at the Women's Centre. Apparently it's eight hours of training every week for eight weeks. I feel she needs to get more support for herself, rather than trying to learn how to support other women in crisis. But as Ania said, rather sternly, in her best education expert voice, often the deepest learning happens obliquely when you don't think about yourself. And maybe she's right. Anyway, at least it gives Leigh some other connections in Brisbane apart from Bill, and an interest other than the midday soaps. I still have trouble stifling the wrap-her-in-eiderdown impulse but she sounded less defeated, a little more animated than when we last spoke. Must curb my impatience. It's just that my desire to see her happy is so pressing!

Bill tells me the life insurance stuff is getting close to being sorted, though we're still not sure how much money's involved. He's keen for me to take all of the pay-out. Says he has all he needs, and he doesn't want to touch the blood money as he calls it. Points out that I'll get it all when he dies, so I might as well have it to enjoy now rather than later. This raises strange and conflicting emotions, as you would guess. Ania and I have had long discussions about it. Some days I want to donate it all to a worthy cause, because I feel it's a lie, no money could compensate for Ruby's death, and I want no part of it. Other days, I imagine how Ruby might have wanted me to use it to do something really different and interesting. Or maybe, if there was enough money we should see about buying an apartment in Sydney, if that's where Leigh ends up studying next year. I just don't know. Bill is utterly certain about not wanting to touch it. Any thoughts from the tropics on this?

Best go, what news of you and your mysterious Katya? Are you going to see her again? Thanks again for the bulging letter, we revelled in it.

Lots of love to you all – Molly.

Dear Molly,

At work it would almost be the end of first semester yet I have no essays or exam papers to mark. You'd think that'd be an unalloyed pleasure but, lobster of habit that I am, I feel oddly disquieted by their absence. Have been unemployed for nearly four months and still find it hard to adjust to the fact. One thing I didn't expect was the way I miss my colleagues, from the really kind and efficient women who ran the office, to the crusty blokes with whom I nearly always disagreed. Guess I enjoyed working together with others to get courses and projects up and running, and even the last-minute crises, the disasters that we always just managed to avert, gave a sense of achievement and satisfaction. It's also been quite poignant to witness the sudden demise of a working team, to hear the stories of how people are managing to put their lives back together after such drastic change. Not many have found work in their fields. These subjects are being lopped off universities all over the country, so the chances of being re-employed elsewhere are not just slim but anorexic. I'm considered one of the fortunate ones because I have an employed partner. And for Angus I am truly grateful. He's been great about not drawing attention to my financial dependence, which hasn't been easy to achieve because I'm super-sensitive about it. Apparently the redundancy packages have all been finalised and we should get payouts next week. Once that's completed I think I'll feel better. Can start doing some serious planning about what I'll try next.

Your dinner sounded wonderful. So happy to hear of you taking some action about the grief — the regret about the unsaid to the now dead is horrible isn't it? And there ain't a damn thing you can do about it except, as you are doing, take precautions so that you don't get caught on the same barbed wire twice. I can imagine Ania really enjoying the pampering. She certainly deserves it.

Not sure about seeing Katya again. She's given me her address in Melbourne, so I guess I could meet up with her if I'm down that way sometime. Tempting to see if she's still as deliciously small and voluptuous as she was ... but perhaps too tempting. I'd hate to go down that complicated path all over again. It was slithery enough the first time! Besides she's got her life all settled, she said it took her quite a while to move on after it all ended. I don't believe that for a minute but ... she was annoyingly vague about whether she had a serious other at present. Hope so, I'd hate her agile fingers and persuasive tongue to be unemployed for too long.

On to other matters, quickly, before I go any further. One thing I've been doing since I've been gifted all this spare time, is to send some of my writing off to journals. I've had one article accepted, as well as a couple of poems, which is pretty satisfying. Have heard there's an interesting Writers' Festival in Brisbane in June, so I'm thinking about going down. A fitting way to spend the first bit of my redundancy package, a gesture towards my hopes of developing the writing as at least one aspect of my new career. Could maybe meet up with Leigh for dinner, if she'd like that. Do you think?

On a hopeful note, met this bloke the other day, who said his union is interested in finding someone to record oral histories of its older workers and then write it up as a small book and was I interested? Well, it may not be as interesting to me as the history of the corset but at least it would be paid work for which I have the right qualifications. So we'll keep talking and see what comes of it. Freelance historian? How does that sound? Though I looked up "freelance" and found it meant a mercenary soldier in medieval Europe. I might like to wear a breastplate on occasions but this doesn't quite sound like me, does it? What about "Independent Researcher and Writer"? Is that sounding better, or too bland and unspecific?

Lola is really well and so happy this year. She adores her teacher, and has discovered the joys of reading. It gives me such pleasure to see her pleasure. So I know what you mean about the imperative to see your children glittering like the surf on a sunny day with happiness. I thought Leigh's option, while not the most obvious way to achieve what you might want, nonetheless is headed in the direction of recovery. At the very least she might make some women friends, and we can hardly think that a bad thing. It's got to be a less dangerous start to her social life than joining a tennis club full of Kevins, isn't it? I was about to say, "You worry too much", but stopped myself in time. It's such a stupid thing to say to any mother. Whilst ever your child's in potential danger you worry, you have to worry. I reckon you must grow the worry gland along with the placenta. Might relieve some of the pressure from Bill too, if Leigh is going out occasionally with someone else. Now don't tell me you're worried she might become a lesbian, mixing with all those stroppy feminists at the Women's Centre, or I'll cry laughing.

Don't know what to suggest about the life insurance money. Bit difficult to say until you know the exact amount. I guess the apartment is a sensible idea in terms of an "investment", but then investing is not something I know a lot about. Wasn't a topic of dinner conversation at home as we scraped by on the Civilian Widow's Pension, as it was called then. Amazing terminology, eh? Imagine Ruby would like you to do something that wasn't sensible with it, something a bit daring and as you say, interesting. I can appreciate Bill's feeling, but I think that if you just hand it on to a charity you'd be avoiding acknowledgment of Ruby's death, and missing an amazing chance to do something distinctive by way of honouring and commemorating her life. It's money from an insurance company, don't forget, and it would be a shame to miss an opportunity to spend their money, wouldn't it? If you wanted to be really subversive you could set up a fund whose sole task was to assist in the legal costs of small claimants who wanted to challenge the decisions of insurance companies. Now that would be worthwhile. Can imagine Ruby giving one of her deep laughs at that idea. But I'm sure you can come up with better ones. Just get creative and think of Ruby's own daring energy.

Better change out of my sarong and into some sensible mother clothes. I promised to take Lola to the library after school and I'd hate to lose my sarong in the middle of the municipal library, especially as it's too hot to wear knickers today. Hope you're continuing to feel gruntled, I would if you were here right now.

Miss you and love you –
Finn

June 6

Dear Finn

Liked the idea of you standing tall as a bare-bummed
goddess, sarong draped elegantly at your feet, in the
middle of the library giving the municipal matrons and
pensioners a real story to tell when they got home. But
I guess Lola wouldn't have been too impressed. Nothing
seems to equal the embarrassment a mother can inflict on
a daughter by daring to step outside the straight mother
role. And I speak from experience – on both sides of the
relationship! Ruby could embarrass me to death just by the
clothes she wore to school functions when I was at high
school. Used to feel as if I'd rolled in a patch of burrs,
I prickled so much, and wondered why, just for once, she
couldn't wear a pastel frock like ALL the other mothers?
Those purple creations she favoured at that stage. I feel the
burrs in my skin even as I write now and its over twenty-
five years ago! Amazing.

The life insurance pay out has come through, along with
all her superannuation. Apparently I was named as her sole
beneficiary. Bill has paid both lots straight into my account.
We had a bit of an argument about it but he says it's
capitalist money, those capitalist insurance bastards can't
pay for Ruby's flesh, and he refuses to touch it. It's an odd
argument but I can sort of see it and arguing with the rage
of the grieving is completely stupid. I know that from
seeing defiant fools sizzle at the end of my own anger.
So there's a huge sum of money suddenly sitting in my
bank and I still don't know exactly what to do with it.
I wondered how Bill would feel about me spending it, but
he says it is mine and he doesn't care what I do, as long as
he isn't involved. Says he won't be resentful if I decide to

keep it rather than give it away. Hope he knows his own emotions. I'd hate this money to affect what we share.

After getting your letter, Ania and I had a long discussion, over coffee, not wine you'll be pleased to hear. Didn't want the jelly woman getting into it, even for a minute. She hasn't a good head for money and careful decisions. Could see what you mean about acting generous to cover my avoidance, and I think you're right. It would be a kind of emotional buck-passing. One thought that your bracing words sparked was that of buying an old house and setting up a Bed & Breakfast establishment. Ania is seriously considering early retirement, she turns fifty-five in January next year as you know. The Education Department is offering attractive packages to encourage staff to do just that. So we're tossing around the idea of running a B&B, either here or somewhere within easy driving distance of Sydney. Depending on the B&B's location, we'd keep this house and I'd be able to run my practice as well as doing the B&B thing part-time. Ania would be the full-time person, and with her vast organisational skills and tact in dealing with lots of different people, I reckon it'd be a winner. It mightn't be the most daring idea but it appeals to both of us and it'd mean we'd spend more time together but not be completely coupled off from the rest of the world. I'm not ready to retire just yet, but because I have flexibility in deciding which hours I work, I can't see why I couldn't combine a small practice with helping to run the B&B. We thought of calling it Ruby's Place. What do you think? I'm quite keen, and think Ruby would like the idea of opening up a whole new lifestyle for Ania and me. You know what she thought about ruts! Only good for burying rubbish in, she used to say.

Would it really be so risky to see Katya again? You seem so bouncy and well-loved living with Angus, and so joyously immersed in Lola, can't see you risking a jot of that hard-won peace for a woman you haven't spoken to for fifteen years. What I do find hard to understand is your sex life. Maybe because I've never been with a man, and have never had even the slightest desire to, I find it tricky to imagine someone who can just go from Katya's bed to Angus's, so to speak, without missing a beat. Is that what you're like? I know a lot of lesbians who go through hetero stuff in a mutilating effort to conform to 'normality', usually when they're young and can't face the fact, and the consequences, of being lesbian. But that doesn't seem to describe you. Am I right? Can you tell me more, or am I being too nosy?

The news from Leigh continues fair. She's made friends with a couple of the other women doing the training course. They've invited her back to their houses a few times. Says she's feeling less fearful and is able to shop by herself now without getting unbearably anxious. Bill sounds relieved. Think he felt right out of his depth – wanting to support her but not knowing how. And there's only so much a grieving grandfather can do. My fingers are crossed, hoping these women can help Leigh get back to her confident, calm self without further trauma. As long as they don't try to seduce her!

Ania and I have an appointment with a money-man this afternoon. Not sure whether it'll be worth the bother but we felt we needed some advice about financial planning! Can't quite believe it, me having finances enough to need planning beyond 'Will there be enough to do the grocery shopping on Friday?', but fate has strange ideas sometimes. Just hope he doesn't push us to invest in shares, because that's one thing I refuse to do with Ruby's money. So at least I've made one firm decision!

If I'm not to be late for that date I'd better stop now and tidy myself up. It's bitterly windy today, so I'll need to do more than change a sarong. How I envy you the easy single layer dressing of the tropics as I slub around looking like the Michelin Man in three or four layers of clothing. Heard the weather forecast for you today, fine and twenty-eight degrees – you lucky warm witch! Hope to hear from you, my Scheherazade, soon –

Lots of love – Molly.

Dear Molly,

Just back from the Writers' Festival, had a really stimulating time. Was great to talk to other writers who struggle along without full-time jobs, and hear some of the creative ways they generate an income. Came back feeling like a ripe seedpod, ready to pop open at the slightest touch. Maybe getting yanked out of the rut wasn't such a dreadful thing. Of course I can only say that now — after how many months of bitterness and rage? Anyway, went to heaps of readings and discussion panels and had lots of serendipitous conversations. Some of the readings were abysmal, Dryden-dull and poorly performed. But in a way they were heartening because I realised that maybe my efforts weren't so pathetic after all.

I struck up a festival camaraderie with a woman called Ester Fredriksen, and we barrelled off to readings together, or went to different sessions and chatted afterwards. Esther had come all the way from Blackall where she runs a small air charter business. She had dared herself to perform a few of her poems sometime during the Festival. A much scarier prospect than doing aerial acrobatics she reckoned. So she had these poems stuffed in her handbag, waiting for the right opportunity. Over a glass of red at a Greek restaurant we decided to put our names down for the open session on the last day, to just give it a go. We gave each other lots of support, saying cheerful things like, "What's the worst that could happen?"; "Well, you could faint and piss your pants and everyone would think it was performance poetry". Anyway we did it (not the fainting!), took it in turns and just read two works each. Later a couple of people from the audience said they really liked our stuff and asked where we were published. That made the sweating fingers and whimpering knees all seem worth while. The unsolicited compliments of complete strangers are somehow profoundly encouraging, aren't they?

As you've no doubt heard, I took Leigh out to dinner at a swisho restaurant in the midst of the festival. Wanted an excuse to wear my best wool pants, and they weren't the kind of thing to wear to the Festival. Casual to grunge was the order of the day there. Also thought it might be good for her to dress up again, seeing the last dress-up occasion ended so horribly. Well, she rose to the challenge like her mother's own daughter, and looked gorgeous in an amber-coloured maxi, with Ruby's necklace gracing her strong neck. She wore the Blundstones underneath. That's a look I love, the contradiction of the elegant cloth and heavy no-nonsense work boots. A lot of my students used to wear it. Apparently Bill was a bit flummoxed, and even suggested Leigh wear a pair of Ruby's purple evening shoes instead. Poor old bugger. Young women these days, I can hear him saying, and shaking his befuddled head!

Anyway, we had a satisfying evening. Was a little awkward at first. It's a long time since we've spent time together without you. Perhaps the last time was when she was ten and you left her with us for a week, while you went to that conference in Hawaii, remember? But the odd feeling of your absence soon eased, you know how accomplished I am at talking. Told her a few anecdotes about you, which she hadn't heard, and then she couldn't help laughing and so we swam into a comfortable current of warmth and stayed there all evening. The food was excellent which certainly helped my mood, and I had forgotten the unsophisticated delight of dessert to the young and hungry! Leigh has retained her robust appetite and I got a lot of pleasure out of watching her enjoy a really beautiful meal. Dropped her back at Bill's at about 10.30, both of us feeling as contented as even you could desire.

Had a whisky with Bill, who'd waited up till Leigh got back. He wasn't taking any chances after last time, he said. He's looking more grizzled than when I saw him last, but still steady in his spry grip on life. We talked vegetable gardens and argued over compost heap methodology till about twelve! Leigh had rolled off to bed by that time and so he was able to tell me some of his anxieties about her, and I think just talking it over with someone outside the family helped him realise that he's doing all the best things and can't do any more. I didn't mention Ruby, felt that grief was too deep and solitary for him to want to share with someone he once knew as a High School stripling. But I enjoyed myself. Thanks for letting me share your family for a bit.

Won't answer your nosy questions, there's no time, and besides it might do you good to have to wait. Also I don't know that I know how to explain any of it to you. Thought the B&B sounded good, though I can't quite see you two as the apple-cheeked upright citizens who usually run such places. Would you think of catering mainly for the gay market? The pink dollar is supposed to be a booming sector of the tourist economy, according to an article I read in a travel magazine on the flight home. Would that make it more interesting and less complicated? Just a feathered thought as I fly.

Will be in touch very soon — love you — Finn

June 27

Dear Finn

A card, to say THANKYOU for taking Leigh out to dinner, and taking the time to talk to Bill. Trust you to thank me for sharing my family with you. The thanks are all due to you, for helping us in such a gentle, subtle way. And damned effective, of course. Leigh rang me the next night and gave me a morsel by morsel description of the meal, said how much you'd made her laugh with your stories about me. But wouldn't tell me which ones. I think I'll have to take Lola out when she's left school and have a similar frank chat! Anyway, apart from the food, Leigh really loved being treated like an equal and there was a wonderful change in her tone of voice, which I attribute entirely to you and your magic healing properties. Now don't go into avoid-the-compliment mode. You just take it on the cheek and accept it for a change. She told me that you told her she was the most beautiful, strong young woman you'd met in a long time. She was quite moved by your good opinion – and of course, as I know you know, the timing couldn't have been better for her. So, before I start to weep over the thought of the two of you, thank you again.

Love for now – and special hugs from Molly.

Dear Molly,

Thanks for the card. It came in the mail with a letter that I've been desperately longing to receive for twenty-two years. A letter telling me news of Carlos. My Carlos, only they called him Sam. This isn't making sense. Can't get control of my thoughts to tell it straight. This is not a cool Scheherazade entertainment. This is the story I've never been able to tell you, or Angus, or anyone. And now I know, at last, his daily real-world name. The one everyone knows him by, everyone who knows how Sam, this Sam, wears his shorts, whether he likes peanut butter, what books he reads, how his shoes wear down, how his arms lie when he's asleep, whether he's a swimmer, if he's silent or a talker, how tall he stands when he wins a prize, whether anyone has ever hit him hard, if he laughs out loud at his favourite television show. Those people all call him Sam, but I called him Carlos for twenty-two years. I've talked to him inside myself, this Carlos, all those years and now he's Sam, and I still don't know if he's really a dark-haired Carlos inside himself or this bright cheeky blonde Sam the rest of the world knows. The rest of some world I know nothing about, and yet I've carried him, this boy Carlos/Sam, inside me all these dreary years of not-knowing. So your card got a bit swamped when I saw the letterhead on this one. I couldn't read anything for ages, couldn't focus under the waves of realising that the not-knowing was ending and I may be about to know some-thing about this baby, this child, this grown man, my son.

I've never written those words to anyone before. My son. My son, Sam. The curled baby, perfect as a tiny bat, I bore the year after I finished school. Sam. Carlos. Which one suits him best, do you think? I don't know. You'd have as much chance of guessing it right as I would. Perhaps he doesn't/wouldn't like either. And yet the lining of my womb knows him, remembers his fluttery first kicks, the steady subtle thrum of his heartbeats and later, his punchy tumble-turns, his poky elbows making mountain peaks dance across my brown unscarred belly. These things I know about him. No one else does. They've never known how he liked to frolic in the warm amniotic sea at two every morning. Or the contemplative frown he wore as he lay in his mother's arms for those first minutes outside the womb. Before they took him away.

The takers away. The givers of sensible advice. The ones who know best, always and forever. Can he ever understand how strong they were? How they hedged me in with their thickets of logic till I couldn't move, couldn't get out of the high-walled maze of 'for your own good and the good of the baby'? They said I wouldn't be able to look after him. Could I? What if I dropped him and killed him? He was so mouse-small and that pulsing blue hole under the skin in his skull. It terrified me. What if something accidentally poked in there and got his brain? I was fierce with wanting to keep him. I was so scared of hurting him. Seesaw. Bewildered. They were thicket-certain. And they knew my fear. They kept saying I couldn't love him as well as someone else. I thought they must be right. So I gave him away to them, to take care of. And curled my Carlos, I named him Carlos to myself, curled him back inside my womb, back to where I had kept him safe all those long-swelling months. In there I'd kept him safe and helped him grow strong lungs and capillaries and legs and eyelashes and every fragile detailed thing, and no one else could love him enough to grow him like that. And he's stayed in there, safe and mine, until now. And now he's Sam. And I know him even less than before, I think. I thought this letter arriving would be the end of not-knowing but it isn't. It's like getting a single peanut to eat when you've been starved. It only makes the fury of hunger worse.

When I was down in Brisbane, I got in touch with the people who link mothers like me with their children and vice versa. They've been very good, and quicker than I thought. So now they've sent me his name, and I can write to him via them if I want to. Of course I want to, but what do you write? Where to start? How do I explain the power of adult righteousness over one bewildered teenager? How to tell him how much I wanted to latch him onto my breast, all aching and lumpy with milk just for him, but they wouldn't let me and took him away and gave him the plastic bottle full of formula when I had the milk all ready and there for him? They said it wouldn't be good for him. Or me. But it hasn't been good for me since the day they took him away. And what's it been like for him? I know I'll never know. Even if I meet him and we talk for 50 years I'll never know so much that I desperately want to know.

Can't write any more.

Molly, write to me and tell me that you, at least, forgive me for giving away my baby. For letting them be so certain. That's what killed my fierceness. Can hear him asking angrily, "How could she?". How can that be answered, understood? Can even you understand? Please write soon.

Love always – Finn

July 17

Finn, my sweet

Want to say straight away that I'm glad, to my very bones,
that you rang the other night. No, you weren't very
coherent, and it was late, but none of that matters. What
matters is that you rang me when you were in pain instead
of trying to pretend you were fine when you weren't. And
no wonder. All those years keeping your profound mother-
pain silent. It's a wonder you're not madder than you are.
So much becomes clear to me now. I do want to thank
you, firstly for writing and then for ringing. And I'm not just
being pleasant or gracious. You know me better than that.

Have you told Angus yet? You must for your sake. You don't
need the pressure of keeping any more secrets. It's too
hard, especially with someone really close. And I can only
imagine that he'd be supportive. Think how good it would
be to lie on his big, solid chest and just rest, instead of
having to keep on carrying this truckload of desperate pain
alone. And if you ever do get to meet Sam then it would be
easier if it were all out in the open. Think you're right not
to tell Lola just yet, though you might need to explain in
general terms that you've just heard some sad news about
someone you knew a long time ago. Just so that she has
some idea why you might be distracted. Being such an
acute observer, and so connected to you, she's sure to
notice you're upset and you don't want to have to pretend
otherwise, any more. No more pretending, I say. It's not
good for your health. Consider yourself told.

There, a whole lot of advice which you probably didn't
want. But you sounded so vulnerable and frantic on the
phone, I feel I have an excuse. Are you doing OK now?
Have you been able to start writing to Sam? Can imagine
you starting fifty-five letters and shredding them all up.

Sure ain't gunna be easy. Perhaps it'd help if you started by writing it all out to me? You know I'm always your keenest reader.

Best away, I have a client just coming down the path, and Ania has promised to post this on her way out. She sends her biggest hugs and says you should ask Angus to cook you that beetroot risotto again. She said she's never known it to fail in the business of soothing wrenched hearts. Look forward to talking with you or hearing from you. You ring anytime, you hear? I'll be really dirty if you don't get me out of bed at least once over this.

I love you and treasure you whatever your secrets, no more talk of forgiveness now – Molly.

July 24

Dear Finn

When I got your message on the answering machine it was
in the middle of a long afternoon and I still had about
three clients to see before I could call you back. Talk about
frustrating. My impatience was rampant. Felt like yelling at
the last appointment. Shouldn't say this, but she's a bit self-
indulgent, keeps bleating about every trivial thing, so she
doesn't ever have time to front up to what she and I both
know is the main game. So I always feel a bit impatient
with her anyway, but add to that my sense of urgency
about calling you back, and I was a shaken champagne
bottle waiting to pop. Still, perhaps urged on by your very
real needs I pushed her harder than usual and I think we
actually did some strong, gutter-clearing work. Course she
may decide never to come back again but at the moment
I really wouldn't care. Seem to have had a marked increase
in new clients in the months since Ruby died. Generally
they've been interesting people with a genuine desire to fix
things, and you know I enjoy working with people like that.

You said that the agency had told you Sam had not
contacted them about wanting to get in touch with you,
but had a current address listed with them and had given
permission for them to release his first name if you asked.
Sounds like he is, or his adoptive parents are, cautious but
not closed-minded. Is that your sense? Could be worse,
couldn't it? Did you go and have that swim after we talked?
Sure sounded like you needed it.

Pleased that you told Angus. Did feel for you, having to
pluck the courage from your badly balding supply. But
sounds like he was understanding, after the initial shock.
When I was talking to Bill last night and telling him a bit
about what you're going through, he said he already knew

about the baby. Old bastard. He's never said a word to me. Makes you wonder what other secrets are locked up in that grizzled great head of his. Had a bit of a go at him for holding back vital info about my best friend and he said he thought it was up to you to tell me when you were ready. So he's been very considerate of you but not so diligent about me. Humph. Guess it must have been common knowledge at the time. Is this what Dave meant at the school reunion when he asked about you and your troubles? Must have been. Gossip of that order doesn't stay hidden in anyone's cupboards in a small country town, does it? Poor you. It must have been hideous. But why was I the last to know? I know, I was out of town, doing my thing at Uni, and not tuning into anything as uncool as home-town news.

Just writing that makes me jitter with questions, but I'll wait till your letter arrives, hoping it will stem my string of what? why? and how?. It's not mere voyeurism, you know that don't you? This is such a huge part of your past, you can understand why I need detail, can't you? Don't go leaving anything out now. Am I setting agendas again? Probably, but Finn, I really need to know the whole story.

Before I go, just a quick bit of news about Leigh. She's been given ten hours of paid work a week at the Women's Centre where she did that course. She'll be on reception, answering calls, giving out info and just being there to look after women who drop in. And one of the other workers has offered to do a trade with her: Leigh's to look after this woman's four-year-old one morning a week and in exchange the woman, Brenda, will give her two hours a week training in Aikido. Apparently it's a Japanese martial art which works on turning your opponent's aggressive energy back onto him. Think I've read about it somewhere. Sounds great. And Leigh sounded excited about both things when I spoke to her last night. Was bloody good to hear some energy back in her voice. She's planning to stay put in Brisbane until the end of the year, come down here round Christmas and then start to get everything set up for uni in the New Year. Sounds pretty damn sensible to me. Just keeping all fingers and toes crossed that nothing complicated happens to throw her off-track.

She's also working with one of Ruby's work friends. They've decided to collect and organise all Ruby's letters and other writings, speeches and so forth. Still a bit unclear about what they'll do with them once they're all collected but there's talk of either a publication or at the very least putting them in a library somewhere. Bill's right in there helping with that, as you would guess. They've been having pizza nights where they all sit round at Bill's place working through bundles of Ruby's stuff, discussing what should go where, drinking red wine and eating pizza. It sounds like a lot of fun and must confess I'm bloody envious that I'm not there with them. Might see about heading up there for a weekend in August. That's the worst month here, weather-wise. Ania and I are sick of being permanently cold and having to lump round in layers and layers of clothing. A weekend lolling under a frangipani by the Brisbane River in a T-shirt would be a great respite from this place. And I'd really like to help with Ruby's stuff. A chance to do something useful with my grief, and honour her in some way.

Maybe all this news seems trivial when I think about what you're facing at the moment. But thought a dose of small news might be a welcome relief. Perhaps news of my child's doings when you're craving news of yours isn't the most tactful thing, but then again my silence won't help the pain of yours, will it? Will be in touch soon –

Love from Molly.

Dear Molly,

It's been a real lifeline to get you on the phone whenever I've needed you these past few weeks. Hate being needy but your generosity has reassured me that it really is okay to be so with you. You'll change the habit of a lifetime yet! Well actually it's more than just one lifetime, it's an inter-generational edict in my family. My mother's motto was "Trouble shared is trouble doubled", and I'm sure she learnt it from her mother, who learnt it from hers, who probably learnt it from hers. So if you can help me unlearn it, then perhaps it won't get passed on as a bitter biscuit to Lola.

Well that went okay, that first paragraph. Been having so much trouble writing anything since finding out about Sam. I'm trying to call him that as a sign to me that this is a real world thing now, not just a fetid internal monologue that has to go on uninterrupted for another twenty years. Still cherish my imagined Carlos but realise that his usefulness is fading as I prepare myself for the possibility of knowing more about, and maybe even meeting, this Sam whom I gave out into the world all those years ago. And of course I know he's different to the baby Carlos, so it seems fitting to use his different name.

There, another paragraph achieved. It's so good to know that you're there to read this. Up until now every time I try to write, it either comes out as complete blobs of gibberish, or in the stiffest schoolgirl-who-has-just-learnt-how-to-make-a-sentence prose. But with you as my reader I feel able to soften up, knowing that whatever mixed up stuff I produce, you'll somehow magically understand it. How come you make me feel that way? Is that why you're such a good therapist? All comes back to the tricky question of trust, doesn't it? And I don't do that easily.

I'm blathering away like your frustrating client, and yes, like her I'm avoiding the crucial story. So no more excuses.

This is going to be hard.

When I was in Year 12 at High School, I started meeting up with some of the teachers at the pub on a Friday night for a few beers. It was fun. We'd argue mightily over the stuff we'd covered at school, the news, school politics, anything was grist for the mill, and I've always loved a good debate, so it was passionate. Felt very adult and special at the time. Heaps more exciting than going to the drive-in with inarticulate boys my own age, whose only interest in me was the chance of a quick grope. One of the single male teachers did a fairly big line for me but I wasn't all that interested. Was keener on ideas and words than romance. Weird even at 17, I guess. The economics teacher was like me, I thought, and he and I would out-argue everyone else. Think he was a bit of a misfit in that place and he missed arguing with people who met him intellectually. So I was a favourite with him. Felt safe with him, he was married, had two little girls, and my mum and I often likened him to an elder brother. Learnt a lot through those discussions and am sure it helped me do really well in the final exams. I certainly sharpened my ability to argue persuasively over all those beers and late nights.

Then one night this teacher kissed me. That combination of intellectual passion and the physical was irresistible. So, a few times after that we did that, kissing and so forth. He was incredibly careful, and mainly went for oral stuff so I didn't run the risk of getting pregnant. I'd never done this kind of thing before. Certainly hadn't featured in the films at the mother-daughter info nights, the sum total of my formal sex education up till then. Was pretty heady stuff sitting astride my economics teacher's face with his nose decorated by the rococo curls of my pubic hair, and his tongue exploring bits of my anatomy I'd only ever read about in biology books. He shouldn't have done this, I know. Now that I understand more about the power dynamics I feel incredibly angry with him. At the time though, I was more than willing. It was the first enjoyable sexual encounter I'd ever had. The first serious one since the abuse. Though in some ways I can see how the first abuse set me up for this. It'd sort of trained me to expect that if a man was affectionate towards me then I'd have to pay for it with sex sometime. The difference in this case was that at least I got some pleasure out of it.

One afternoon we stupidly did the full bit, he withdrew at the last minute. This was about two months before the HSC. So when my bleeding was late I didn't get too panicky, thought it was just the stress of final exams. We both got such a fright that day though, that we never did anything sexual again. We didn't realise it was too late. Wasn't till the exams were all over and December hit and still there was no bleeding that I got really worried. And yep, I was pregnant. So that's how Carlos began.

Mum was furious. She'd trusted that teacher and I'd ended up in the worst pregnant teenage-girl cliche ever. He was remorse-ridden but didn't want to upset his marriage and kids. Neither did I. I'd enjoyed the debating and the sex with him, but I definitely didn't want to live with him forever. He offered to pay for an abortion, and that was mum's favoured solution too, but by the time we looked into it, it was past the first trimester. Too late for that quick fix. In a way I was relieved. Hadn't been keen on the abortion idea myself. I mean, I could see the rational argument, but my body was arguing differently.

So it had to be a full-term pregnancy and some part of me was ecstatic about growing a new life. That gave me a real buzz every time I thought of it. Had to be a secret pleasure, of course. Everyone else was determined to define the whole scene solely as "a problem". And that's when the maze of hedges began to grow up around me. The logic. The defining of me as incompetent. And how could I argue? I didn't know if I could be a good enough mother, I'd never done it before. But I didn't want to give him up either. They won in the end. I never breastfed him. Cruelty dressed up as care, all for "the best". Never a moment's question about whose best we were discussing. Maybe they were right. My life certainly would have been utterly different but I'll never know, and nor will Sam, whether that different life would have been harder than the ones we got shunted into by the takers away. Is it any wonder I get anxious about giving advice?

Better go. I'm supposed to be meeting a group of union blokes in a pub, the ones who're interested in doing an oral history of their workers. Think I mentioned it to you once before. They got the grant they applied for, so we're meeting to see what they have in mind and whether I'm the right woman to do it. Have some doubts myself, but who knows? Could be a good distraction from all these memories. And even more important, some sort of income for a while.

Tell Leigh I'm really pleased about her news. Is she going to continue to live with Bill? Could send her some info on archiving if she wants any for the project involving Ruby's papers. But I must have a shower and try to look normal. Haven't even tried to read this over. So excuse any stupid bits. It's hard enough getting it out without trying to tidy it up. I can't.

Love you — Finn

August 16

Dear Finn

Phew, what a tale. Certainly not one I could whip through whilst sipping a genteel G&T. Made me so angry. Think I can guess which teacher it was. Hard to believe someone so supposedly 'nice' could be such a downright sleaze. But you didn't name names. Why not? Is it still just too painful? I hope you're not mistakenly concerned with protecting his 'good name'. Are you? Firstly he doesn't have one, as far as I'm concerned. And secondly, he bloody doesn't deserve protection! What a first-rate bastard, ripping you off like that. I don't care, even if you'd tried to tear his jeans off a dozen times, which you didn't, he had no excuse. He knew what he was doing, and he knew he shouldn't. Talk about taking advantage. Hope he caught a particularly nasty strain of herpes from the next girl he tried it on, and has been suffering ever since. Did he tell his wife? Did you? Did they stay together?

What happened after that? You will tell me the rest soon, won't you, please? Did you stay home with your mum through the pregnancy (can't bear to use that word 'confinement') or go some place else?

How did the meeting with the unionists go? Can just imagine you tossing a few beers back and charming the thongs off them. And of course you're the right woman for the job. Talented broad like you. They'd be lucky to have you agree to do it. So none of this false modesty next time, missy.

Life here is pretty normal and steady, and for that I feel thoroughly grateful. After all the events of the past year, I'm really happy to be bored for a change. Is that what your 'Away with Espalier' poem was about? Had a bit of trouble understanding it when you first sent it, but stumbled across it when I was cleaning up my bedside table the other day, and re-read it and suddenly thought, now I get it! I'm a bit slow sometimes.

Ania and I have been pottering around real estate agents with a view to this B&B idea. Nothing extraordinary has grabbed us but it's good to get a sense of how much you might have to pay for what. Serves to limit the fantasy a bit though. Prices are incredible. And I'd forgotten how delightful real estate agents could be. Was tackled by one as I was reading his window the other day. He reminded me of Joe Kirkham, same sausagey skin and sportsman-run-to-seed style. Wearing the groovy, tight polo shirt with shorts and long socks to show off the muscles, except they've all turned into solid fat. Couldn't extricate myself fast enough. But he was one of those blokes who, as soon as you show that you want to be off, feels compelled to keep you talking for another ten minutes. Wouldn't buy a box of tissues from him even if I had the worst head cold in history – let alone a house!

We're also idly discussing going to Brisbane again, perhaps the weekend after next. Really missing Leigh, and Bill could do with a daughterly dinner or two I suspect. Plus there's the attraction of heading north to where it's warmer. Ania reckons it might be better to wait till her next lot of school hols and then we can cruise rather than rush it. Don't know yet. Arguments both ways. What about you? Got any plans for a trip south, to give your winter clothes an airing? You know we'd both love to see you, anytime. And what news of Lola? Has she cottoned on to your upset yet? Hope it wasn't a difficult one to handle. You absolutely don't need any of those right now. Maybe Angus can field some of it for you?

Will away to chop some wood for the fire. The currawongs are just starting to sing down the dusk (as you would say) and the cold is starting to grab my ankles. A brisk walk and woodchop will get me hungry for Ania's pumpkin and prawn soup. Think she's even baked some bread. She's a marvel that woman. Hope you're having something nourishing to feed your soul tonight too. Missing you heaps. Would be fun to sit round being bored together. Except life with you never is.

Love you, and miss you, and can't wait to get your next – Molly.

Dear Molly,

Still haven't written to Sam. Have tried a zillion times but hate them all. I don't want him to hate me. That's the gristle of it. But I have no power over that, I know. I tell myself there's no rush, but still can't help feeling kind of breathless with anxiety, as if I'm neglecting to do something incredibly urgent. Having nightmares. Angus's chest is just about worn out from being lain on in the middle of the night. Luckily the weather's not too hot for body contact yet.

As you rightly guessed the meeting with the unionists went well. So they're paying a large portion of the grant into my bank account and I'll start work on it next week. It will stop me obsessing about Sam I think, and I'm looking forward to interviewing a lot of these old guys and their families. Might just slip in the odd question about violence both at work and at home, could give me the material for separate paper. Or is that too greedy? Can see I'll have to wrestle with my conscience on that one.

I know, I know, I'm supposed to finish telling the story. I do think it's helping, even though I was a blubbering wreck the day after writing my last one. So (deep breath) the pregnancy had to run full-term and then there was the question of where I'd live while growing my baby. I was keen to stay at home. I didn't feel ashamed of anything. Compared to the humiliation of the earlier abuse this felt like nothing. But the teacher was keen for me to be out of sight. Suspect he didn't want me living close enough to be able to call round to his place some balmy night and drop him in it. He suggested I go to stay with his sister who had a big house in Brisbane near the uni, and a spare room she liked to rent out to students, to help pay off her mortgage. And this is the hardest bit — mum wanted me to go away too. Impossible to describe how that made me feel. She was ashamed of me, wanted me completely out of her life, I was an embarrassment. This hurt more than anything else in the whole sorry business. Never quite forgave her. We hardly spoke in the year after I left home. There were a few strained phone calls after the birth, I called her a couple of times when I was overseas, and a few more times when I redeemed myself as her good little girl and went off to uni. And three months after I started uni she was dead. No chance to resolve anything. The questions I've wanted to ask her, questions that etched themselves into my skin, about why and how — and they're unanswerable and, of course, unanswered. If I ever get cancer, look inside the tumour and those questions will be clustering at the core like hungry maggots.

So, feeling about as powerful and connected to the world as a comatose goldfish in a glass bowl I was freighted off to Brisbane to live with this complete stranger. She was nice enough in a remote kind of way, thought her brother was being very compassionate to one of the girls in his class who'd got herself into trouble. The impulse to vomit out the truth to her was so strong. But I didn't. Think my survival mechanism in those days was to shut down certain parts of my body and brain, so they couldn't sense the full assault of what was happening. To say those months were lonely would be a pallid nonsense. Had to keep the house spotless to pay a portion of the rent for my room. The teacher paid his sister a peppercorn amount. But I survived. Spent a lot of time talking and singing to Carlos. Did lots of things I thought would help me to grow him strong and healthy. Did miles of swimming. And walking. And then there was the birth. And then they took him away.

I stayed in Brisbane a couple of months after that. Had the check-up to make sure I was all okay inside. They said I was but I feel like that huge ripping wound has never healed properly. And then I caught a bus to Adelaide, where I knew absolutely no one. Got myself a job in a cafe. Worked long hours for five months. Saved every cent I could. Then flew to London and worked there for over a year. That's when I met my first woman lover. Then came back one January with a view to starting my uni course. I'd been accepted into one straight after the HSC but deferred because of Carlos.

That's about it I guess. Find I simply can't write about the birth itself.

Love to you and Ania from — Finn

September 10

Dearest Finn

My love, what a bleak time. Have often wondered about
what happened between you and your mum but thought it
was all to do with her death. Didn't realise the rift
happened before that. Like you, I find myself asking,
'How could she?' But she's not around to tell us her side of
the story. She always seemed so strong and open-minded.
Suppose even the strong have things they can't deal with.
But she's beyond my sympathy now, it's you I feel for.
Those awful months waiting for the birth and then working
in Adelaide. All that walled up grief. That degree of
isolation. Gather you didn't ever talk to anyone about it,
until now. Is that right? What an incredible feat of not-
talking for an articulate woman. Want to climb on the next
plane, tuck you into bed, and keep you there for a week,
feeding you every comfort food I can dream up. We must
find a way to get together soon. What are your Christmas
plans? This is too hard for you to revisit by yourself. I know
Angus is there and he's pretty good, but no one's as good
as a Molly for a needy you. That's modest, isn't it? But
totally true.

At present we've put our Brisbane trip on hold. Rang Leigh
and Bill last week and got a pretty clear message about
staying away. Everything is running smoothly up there and
they both seemed to think I might upset the balance.
Felt a bit hurt, as you can imagine, but when I got over
that, I could sort of see their point. You know when you've
just achieved some sort of calm after a calamity, how you
feel that even something good will threaten it if strong
feelings are going to be stirred. At least that's what I think
they mean. And I'm such an organiser, I can understand
their doubts. I'd been thinking that I'd have to be careful,

especially round the issue of the Ruby archive. But apparently I don't have to be careful. I just have stay clear. Humph. And sigh. Glad Leigh is so independent and clear about stuff, and trusts me enough to say these things, but still ...

We're still trying to decide what we'll do for the next lot of school hols. I'd be up to visit you like a flash, if you'd only say you need me. But saving that, the most popular idea is to fly to NZ for ten days to stay at some up-market B&B's I've read about. It's only so we can see how it's done, in the nature of market research, you understand. I'm sure we won't get a minute's pleasure out of feeding on the best fresh produce and quaffing the best NZ wines. Actually it'd be piggish bliss. And our first ever proper holiday alone. Imagine being able to have an utterly adult holiday for a change, where you can stay in bed all day if you want, without that frantic pressure to do things because your hyperactive kid has to be out and doing. The number of train rides, and games of 'I spy', and early morning swims in icy water, and trail rides on miserable skinny ponies, and episodes of Sesame Street, and shopping expeditions to teenage clothes and music outlets, do I need to go on? Sometimes I'd groan but still quite enjoy it, especially if Leigh got a buzz from doing whatever it was. But the freedom to holiday how we want – it'd be so good. Might even be time for some long slow sex. Wouldn't that be a revelation?

Have just read over that and realise how stupid and insensitive it sounds in the face of all the holidays you've never had with Sam. Every time I look at my life, the depth of your loss winds me. Stuff we take for granted, and grizzle about happily, looks so different from where you're standing. Must have made Lola's birth a double-edged blessing. She must have felt so precious, a baby you could keep, but everything you loved about her would make you realise all the more intensely what you'd missed out on the first time. How have you borne it? How does any mother survive whose baby is forcibly removed by do-gooders or death? Having survived my mother's death, I'm not sure if I could survive Leigh's. The injustice would just be too huge. And yet you're living proof it can be done, with style and generosity. Have I told you that I think you're a pretty wonderful woman? Well now I have. Finn, I miss you terribly. Every time I think of you as that aching teenager, living in cheap digs, talking to no one, bravely going on because you were too stunned to think what else to do, cut off from your mum and anyone you'd ever loved. It brings tears to my eyes. Want to go back in time and fix it, make it all come out right, instead of so grim. Is there anything a friend can do, now, to help? If there is, no matter if you think it's too big, please ask it anyway.

Love you – Molly.

Dear Molly,

Was great to get your letter. There's nothing you can do to help except what you already do, and have done for years and years, to write and ring, to make me laugh, occasionally tell me that I'm wonderful and tell me your life. That's what's made a difference and made me better, silkier. I have no ask of you, except that you stay the same. Well, no, I don't expect that you'll stay exactly the same, that'd be just too boring but ... oh, you know what I mean.

Isn't this a great picture of a bowl of mulberries? Reminded me of the mulberry raids we did as kids. I wonder whether Sam has ever eaten mulberries? I remember sitting up in those big old trees in the backyard for whole dreamy days, emerging from their green light looking like purple-mouthed gremlins, with mitts to match. Is your tree fruiting yet? I forget what time of year they crop in the mountains. Tell me you're harvesting them by the bowlful and I'll be on the next flight with a packet of icing sugar in my backpack.

Not space for a long one. Am feeling a bit less shaky about Sam. Perhaps the catharsis of writing it out for you. Don't know. Have drafted a letter to him. Now to try to pick out a suitable photo of his mother. Aargh!

Thanks for being there — that's all I really need.

Love — Finn

Dear Molly,

The card got stuck in Angus's bag. He forgot to post it. Anyway after I discovered this irritating fact I thought I'd open it up again and add a bit more. Have been thinking about you so much lately, and longing to feel you near.

My strength is an illusion. It was good to tell you the Carlos story but if I thought that'd end the pain I was totally kidding myself. Think it's probably the start of some sort of healing but it's going to be a bloody long process. I'd become so clever at burying this and other disasters. Sometimes I still wonder whether repression isn't actually the best idea. Letting it all out HURTS. There are still so many questions I need answers to. They're as urgent as a swarm of cranky bees. Can't sleep much. The bees buzz out at 3 a.m. and frenzy around the bed, stinging every available soft spot with their vicious whys and hows. It's bloody hopeless, and exhausting.

One thing I need advice on is what do I tell Sam about his father? Should I contact the bastard and let him know what's going on? I've lost touch with him, but I'm pretty sure the old school would have his current address. Or the Dept of Education would tell me, maybe. What do you think? The thought of talking to him makes me feel nauseous. Stupid isn't it? It's so long ago but the wound is still fresh. An amazing example of mummification. Dig down through 3000 layers of repression, open up the wrappings and it's all still there, as savage and tender as ever. Great. For myself, I wouldn't talk to the prick, but won't Sam want to know about *both* his parents?

But of course I'm leaping way ahead of myself. Sam may not get in touch even when I do send the letter, so I might be torturing myself about this stuff for nothing. What will I do if I twist myself up enough to send the letter, with a few pathetic photos and then nothing comes back? Silence again. Not sure if I can bear that. It was such a long time of not-talking, not-looking at this, and now I have faced it, what if there's no response? Back to deathly blankness all over again. Molly, that possibility sends me lurching round to thoughts of final picnics again. Please, tell me how to live through this. I can't talk to Angus about how I'm feeling. And I know I shouldn't think like this at all when I have Lola ...

I'd better re-read some of your strong-woman letters to claw myself out of this evil pit. Please write soon. Having peeled back the mango cheek, the worms are threatening to take over. Perhaps I shouldn't send this, but I think I need to. I need you.

Love always — Finn

Dear Molly,

Just saw this postcard when I was out doing some urgent shopping (of the toilet paper and onions kind) so thought I'd write quickly just to let you know how much I relish you right now. How did my mother survive her life without a woman friend like you? Thank you, thank you for the long phone call. It was just the tonic I needed. The mood fluctuations have been bloody incredible. Sorry to burden you with them. But you did say to yell when I was hurting, so I did. And you eased me back to safe space with your gentle parachute silk strength.

Love you and thank you — Finn

October 11

Dear Finn

Your postcard caught us just as we were flinging the bags
into the airport shuttle bus. I read it on the plane and it
added extra tonic to the gin I was sipping.

NZ is wonderful. Ania and I are pampering ourselves,
though we're doing small amounts of bushwalking and
swimming as well, you'll be pleased to hear. Yesterday we
swam in a river made from melted glacier. A real heart-
starter that one. Ania bet that I couldn't swim across it, and
you know what a sucker I am for a dare? Anyway I did it,
but my nipples felt like stalagmites of ice afterwards. Ania
did a sterling job of warming them up though.

We've stayed in about five different B&Bs. They've been
great, but talking to the people who run them has put us
right off buying one. So much effort to live in a house and
have it so meticulously clean and tidy and well-maintained
ALL the time. All that fussing around with bed linen and
crispy white towels and paint. And you have to be at home
all the time. I enjoy it when someone else provides it, but
can I get motivated to do it myself? I don't think I'm cut out
for it. So it's back to the drawing board for plans for Ruby's
money. Out of space – love you – will call as soon as we
get back – Molly.

Dear Molly,

Glad to hear NZ was all you hoped it would be ... and that this first childfree holiday was as satiating for you and Ania as you dreamt it would be. Can see what you mean about the B&B set-up. I know you've had to keep your place pretty pristine since you've been working at home but just letting people walk down your front path, into the front room for an hour and then off again is rather different to letting them actually live in your space. Was Ania as turned off the whole plan as you were? Can imagine lengthy and perhaps inflamed discussions over a bottle or two of NZ wine if you reacted differently to these possibilities. Have you thought of something else to do with all that unexpected money? Do tell.

And what news of Leigh and Bill at present? Are they still slowly recovering, or should I say learning to live differently, after all the difficult bits life has thrown at them in recent times?

Me, I'm finding a lot of my energy is spent plugging the many rents and splits in the hull of my coracle of grief but I do try to raise my face from all the seeping and downright flooding to present a smiling mother and woman-of-the-world face to those around me. Angus is being as supportive as he possibly can while not really understanding how keelhauled I feel. Sometimes it's such an effort to show the proper degree of interest in his lengthy tales of workplace politics and skulduggery. My mind keeps drifting off to thoughts about Sam and what kind of person he is ... would he be as petty and territorial as some of Angus's colleagues? Lola doesn't follow at all though she does a great line in bringing me glasses of water and her favourite teddy bears on the rare occasions when she finds me crying. Equally though I find her exuberant energy a great distraction and solace. It's impossible to stay curled in the bottom of the damp coracle when she puts on her latest hits album full volume and invites me to dance. A few minutes rioting round the living room in the late afternoon sun watching the way her hair rhythms with the rest of her generous body (her curves remind me of mounds of creamy meringue) absorbs and restores me so vehemently. I just wish and bleakly wish I'd had the chance to know Sam this way. Wonder if he's a dancer, or could have been if I'd been able to ... No, I'm not going to go there.

The other distraction for me at present is this union oral history. Have done a lot of the background research and a couple of interviews. I felt I needed to do more research (most of the archives are in Brisbane and Melbourne) before interviewing but there is a sense of urgency because a lot of the key blokes are getting old and developing serious health problems. So there's a real risk of them dying before I can get their stories down on tape. Anyway, I interviewed one of these blokes last week. Joe's 86 and is in the early stages of lung cancer but still comes across as a stroppy great Alsatian of a man. He's been a real mover and shaker in the union ever since he joined it when he was in his teens. He and I had a great old rave up after his initial suspicions were whittled away by me supplying a judicious amount of XXXX to help proceedings along. After our second session he got on the blower (as he said) to one of his mates down in Sydney, who just happens to be the union's NSW state president. The end result of all that is that Joe persuaded his mate, Ted, that the union should commission me to write a full-length book based on oral histories of union members from all around Australia. Ted's been on the blower to his federal colleagues and discussions are under-way, as they say. Joe's ill health has made them see the urgency of doing something fast.

I am pretty keen. It'd be an absolutely huge job but I'm not exactly overwhelmed with other jobs at the moment and I do love the whole process of interviewing ... the way you can find out all this hidden but fascinating stuff when you sit someone down in front of a tape-recorder and ask them about their lives. You hear all the stuff they think is trivial but reveals so much about the era, the mind-set, the accepted mores. It'd mean a fair bit of travel but I think it'd be manageable ... though it would give me opportunities to look up Katya that perhaps I could do without! That might cost me a wrestle with my conscience on a couple of occasions. Whatever, I'm rapidly writing up a costed proposal for the book and will send it off next week. Have decided to be up-front and propose that at least one chapter look at the stories of the unionists' families ... reckon the wives and kids would have some terrific tales to contribute too. We'll see how that goes down. If they like the proposal and don't baulk at the expense, I'll fly down for a meeting in either Sydney or Melbourne sometime in the next month, depending on where their next federal executive meeting is being held. I've got all my fingers and toes crossed that it's in Sydney so I can easily slide up the mountains and visit with you. It would be so good to see you and Ania. Will let you know when things become more certain.

Still haven't written to Sam. Wouldn't it be kinder to just leave him in peace? What if he isn't the least bit interested in the dumb broad loser who gave birth to him? He might be happily immersed in being a lively young bloke who doesn't want to think about anything other than handling himself well at work, buying his first car, spending time with his mates, seeing how his sports' team goes in the comp, and when he'll get his next lay. Shouldn't I put his needs before mine instead of going trampling in with all my violent desires for intimacy, upsetting whatever rosy applecart he and his real family have set up? I mean I'm just the womb, the dumb flesh that grew the foetus that later developed into this complex human being known as Sam ... and that simple piece of basic animal biology doesn't make me his family in any sense at all, does it?

You can see what I mean about the fluctuations. But I set myself the task of not writing about Sam in this letter. Failed on that score I guess, but no more on that right now. Am edgy excited about the possibility of visiting my Molly soon. Would you be able to wangle any free days if I stayed down after the meeting? But I get ahead of myself, there may not even be a meeting yet.

Best away, Lola is having a sleepover Saturday night so we're going shopping this afternoon after school for lollies, chips, coke and videos to keep them all hyperactively entertained ... the things parents get leg-roped into! Hope we all survive with some degree of sanity even if sleep is impossible. Next house I live in must have a giggle-proof bedroom for Angus and me.

Love to you and Ania
Finn

November 12

Dear Finn

Just a quick note to let you know that Ania and I have
already started ironing the sheets and planning the feasts.
What do you mean there mightn't be a meeting? Of course
there bloody will be. They'd be mad not to get a brilliant
historian like you onto this project pronto, and I bet,
knowing you, that your costings were more than
reasonable. It'd be a bloody bargain, which I'm sure those
crafty unionists will see in a flash. By the way I'm really
pleased that this project has come your way, you're a clever
woman and more people should get to know it. In fact
though, Ania and I decided over our second whisky last
night (well, it's one way to honour Ruby's memory!) that
meeting or no meeting we want you to come for a pre-
Christmas visit anyway. So get packing and organising.

I'm pretty flat out this week (hence the card rather than a
long letter) but given a bit of notice I can and will set aside
some client-free days so that I can take you out for long
lunches and short bushwalks but most of all make time for
those unfettered talks with you that I've been so hungry for
(voracious even) lately. I said before that I felt what you
needed most of all right now was a Molly and I still believe
it would be the best thing for you ... not that I have a
vested interest in thinking that way, of course! So please,
let's start talking dates? What about the first week of
December? Look in that diary of yours and I'll bet there's
nothing in that week so pressing that it couldn't be
rearranged to make way for a week of totally indulgent
Molly-coddling for my poor aching Finn? There isn't, is
there, huh?

I know, I'm being bossy and pushy but it is what you need,
I know. Come down and let me look after you. I guarantee

the fluctuations about Sam will ease (I didn't say stop). You can help us work out a sensible plan for Ruby's inheritance. I'm sure Lola and Angus would be OK without you for ten days or so and you'd still get back up north in time to go to all those end of school concerts and presentations which rash up the middle of December for every parent in Australia. Come on, Finn, you know it's the perfect plan. I get all palpitated just thinking about picking you up from the airport and bringing you up here to sleep in Leigh's bed ... bringing you breakfast on a tray mid-morning and then languidly easing you off to a wicked lunch followed by a nap ... ah, I know you're tempted now.

Look forward to getting the dates and flight numbers soon ... and that's more than a gentle hint ... I do miss you so.

Love always — Molly.

Acknowledgments

For permission to reproduce the extracts included in this work, acknowledgement is made to the following publishers and authors.

For works by this author which appeared in previous publications (in a slightly different form):

Scant Publishing, Melbourne for 'Cartwheeling' from *Sexuality: An Anthology of Erotica*, edited by Megan Surmon, 2001;

Five Islands Press, Wollongong University, for the poems 'Cartwheels'; 'Breasts'; 'Toad's Tongue'; 'Away with Espalier'; 'The Kali in Me'; 'The Gift Arrives'; 'She's At School'; 'First Wound'; 'A Glass of Water and a Bed with Clean Sheets'; 'I turn on you I burn you up'; and 'In Katya's Room' from *The Ocean in the Kitchen*, by Gina Mercer, 1999.

For works by other writers:

MacMillan, London, for 'Neutral Tones' by Thomas Hardy, 1867, from *Poems of Thomas Hardy,* edited by T.R.M. Creighton, 1974 (p. 26).

University of Queensland Press, St Lucia, for the extract from *The Vigilant Heart*, by Catherine Bateson, 1998 (p. 11).

Judy Horacek for cartoon no. 35 from *Unrequited Love: Nos 1–100: Cartoons by Judy Horacek*, published by McPhee Gribble Publishers, Ringwood, 1994.

Karen Attard for the poem 'the four men behind her' from *Whisper Dark 3,* 1995 (p. 24), Five Islands Press, Wollongong University.

Adele Horin for 'The Secret Circle' from *Mother Love: Stories about Births, Babies & Beyond,* edited by Debra Adelaide, 1996 (pp. 167–78), Random House, Milsons Point.

Readers may be interested in full details of the books mentioned by Molly and Finn:

Audre Lorde, 'Uses of the Erotic: The Erotic as Power', in *Sister Outsider: Essays & Speeches,* The Crossing Press, Freedom, 1984 (pp. 53–9).

Myra Jehlen, 'Archimedes & the Paradox of Feminist Criticism', in *Signs, 6: 4,* 1981 (pp. 575–601). Reprinted in *Feminisms: An Anthology of Literary Theory & Criticism* (Revised Edition), Edited by Robyn R. Warhol & Diane Price Herndl, MacMillan Press, Basingstoke, 1997 (pp. 191–212).

Cora Kaplan's Introduction to *Elizabeth Barrett Browning's Aurora Leigh,* Women's Press, London, 1978 (p. 36).

Germaine Greer, *The Change: Women, Aging and the Menopause,* Hamish Hamilton, London, 1991.

Janet Frame, *The Envoy from Mirror City: An Autobiography,* Volume 3, Hutchinson Group, Auckland, 1985 (pp. 103–4).

If you would like to know more about Spinifex Press,
write for a free catalogue or visit our Home Page.

SPINIFEX PRESS

PO Box 212, North Melbourne, Victoria 3051   Australia
http://www.spinifexpress.com.au